The
Widening River

Hope you
enjoy it !
Hazel

The
Widening River

— HAZEL HUTCHINSON —

Published by Northsea Publishing

A CIP catalogue record for this book is available from the British Library.

ISBN 978-1-7399814-1-9

Book layout and cover design by Clare Brayshaw

Prepared and printed by:

York Publishing Services Ltd
64 Hallfield Road
Layerthorpe
York YO31 7ZQ

Tel: 01904 431213

Website: www.yps-publishing.co.uk

CHAPTER ONE

A Visit

Icould never have imagined that a single encounter would turn my life upside down. There was something almost familiar about him from the start, as if I'd met him long ago. But I was certain that I hadn't.

"Excuse me, but are you Helen Johnson?" Surely, he could have seen the name badge I was wearing, so I don't know why he had to ask. Maybe he was short-sighted. He certainly seemed to be peering at me most intensely. Or maybe he couldn't read. Even though I worked in a library, I came across plenty of older people who struggled with reading and writing. They used to bring me letters to read for them, usually from the council. "Only I wondered if I might have a word with you when you've got a minute."

I glanced at the clock. Quarter to one. "Can you give me fifteen minutes?"

He sat down. I was aware of him looking in my direction from time to time, passing his hand over his short grey hair, polishing one shoe against the other ankle. His shoes were scuffed, down at heel. He was dressed in a suit, but it was shabby, as if he'd had it for years and it was the only one he owned.

"Okay," I said, once I'd finished for lunch. "How can I help you?"

"Sorry to bother you at work, love, but I was trying to get in touch with your mam. Your neighbour said I'd find you here."

"Oh. Didn't she tell you? I'm afraid my mum passed away. A couple of years ago."

He paused, and again he seemed to be looking at me, trying to work something out.

"Sorry love, I didn't know that. I saw her picture in the paper, and I thought I'd maybe come and see her."

"In the paper? When?"

"Well, it were a few years ago I suppose. There was a flood."

"That was two thousand and seven. Six years ago!"

"Aye well, I wasn't sure. I didn't know whether to get in touch or not. Anyway, I don't suppose it matters now. Sorry, love. Sorry for your loss."

"It's okay. Did you want to see her about something in particular?"

"No, no, not really. She was an old friend, you see. I just thought I'd come to Hull and look her up."

"She might've mentioned you. What's your name?"

"Steve. Steve Henderson. Only she didn't know me as Steve. I was called Jim back then."

"Jim? No, the only Jim she mentioned was my dad."

"Your dad." He paused, for a long time. His pale eyes seemed to focus on mine and then on something in the distance, as if his thoughts had turned in on themselves. Wherever he had gone, I wasn't sure I could follow. I waited. Then, in a voice that seemed to belong to someone else, he spoke. "How old are you, Helen, if you don't mind me asking?"

"Funny question. But since you ask, I'm thirty-eight, well nearly thirty-nine. It's my birthday tomorrow actually."

"So, you were born in … seventy-four?"

"Yes, you've obviously got a good head for figures. Though I don't see why you're so fascinated by my age. I'm sorry, but I don't even know who you are."

Another pause. Now he was looking at me directly.

"I think I'm your dad, Helen."

And that was when I knew he was a fraud. Or a lunatic. Because my dad died years ago. In nineteen seventy-four, in fact.

CHAPTER TWO

A Conversation

I told him to go away, to get lost or I'd call the police. And he left, didn't say another word. But then, all afternoon, I couldn't stop thinking about what he'd said. Why would he have claimed to be my father?

I knew my dad had lost his life in a trawler accident, but Mum had never talked about him very much. When I'd asked her about him, she'd said he was nice, but she hadn't known him that long, and then he was gone. And then I'd come along. Her mum, my nan, had helped bring me up. We'd been a family of women for as long as I could remember.

I'd asked her again, when she was becoming really ill, and I knew there wasn't much time left. It was as if I'd wanted to hang onto what remained of my disappearing family. "How long did you know my dad for, Mum?"

"The thing is," she said, "we weren't exactly going out with each other. It was more of what you'd call a one-night stand. He was married, you see." She laughed. "Makes me sound like a bit of a slapper, doesn't it?"

"Bit of a pattie-slapper, were you Mum?"

"No, love. That's what we used to call the lasses that worked in the fish factories."

"Didn't you ever do that, Mum?"

"What? Work in fish factory? No chance."

"I thought you lived on Hessle Road."

"Aye, but there's no way your nan would've let me work in a factory. Though I could've done with the cash."

"What did you do, then?"

"Why, I learnt to type and do shorthand. And I got a job in the bank. It was on Hessle Road, mind. The Yorkshire Bank. Beautiful building. The girls I was at school with used to call me Miss Snooty, but they didn't mean it really. We still had a laugh. We used to go out on a weekend, in our mini-skirts, dressed up to the nines."

"I thought it was all headscarves and prams on Hessle Road."

"Well, it wasn't long before it was. For most of them anyway."

"What about you? Didn't you say you got engaged once?"

"Aye, but your nan put her foot down."

"Why?"

"Because he was on trawlers. Like your grandad was. And your dad, for that matter. And that was the year that three of them went down in one month. And your nan said it was no life being a trawlerman's wife."

"So, what did she want you to do?"

"I think she just wanted me to do a bit better for myself."

"Didn't you mind her telling you what you could and couldn't do?"

"Well, it did get on my nerves, a bit. But I didn't really want to move out. You see, my dad wasn't always very nice to be around. He was all right with me, but he could turn a bit nasty when he'd had a drink. I kind of wanted to be there for your nan. Not that she couldn't look after herself. She's a tough old bird, you know."

"But you did move out, didn't you?"

"Aye, after they moved us out to Northfield. Your nan was all excited about getting a bathroom, but no way was I going to live on some godforsaken estate."

"So, what did you do?"

"Well, I moved into a flat on Boulevard with one of my mates, and we were like the Liver Birds, but from Hull, not Liverpool. A right pair of dolly birds. You should've seen us when we got tarted up to go out. We had a right laugh, the two of us. And then I had you. And that was that."

"You make it sound like it was the end of the world."

"Of course, it wasn't. Come here, love."

And I'd gone over to her and given her a hug. It had to be a gentle one, because she was so thin, already.

Mum was small and fair, like me. The funny thing was, you could still see what she'd been like when she was a dolly bird. I've heard it said that everyone keeps to the look they had when they were twenty. Her blond shoulder-length hair was a throwback to the nineteen-sixties: bouffant on top and flicked out at the ends. Only now it was a wig, after the chemo.

That was the last time we'd talked about my dad. And that was fine because it was all I needed to know just then. But two years later, I suddenly had a lot of questions to ask.

Who was the man she'd been engaged to? And who was my father? And who was the man I'd just met?

CHAPTER THREE

Delving into the Past

It was a quiet afternoon in the library, and I couldn't put the questions out of my mind, so I decided to do a bit of research.

It wasn't difficult to find information on the internet about lost trawlers. Even I had heard about the triple trawler disaster in 1968 when three Hull trawlers were lost in less than a month. I read the last message from the captain of the Ross Cleveland, which went down on February 4th:

I am going over. We are laying over. Help me. I am going over. Give my love and the crew's love to the wives and families.

As I reread his words, I could almost feel the icy blast of the wind. I shivered. I'd never cried for my dad, because I'd never known him, but I suddenly felt this enormous sense of loss. I thought of those families waiting for news of their husbands, fathers, sons, and then finding out that their ship had gone down. I imagined the despair of the crew as the storm and blizzard raged and as the ice built up on the ship. And that final moment as it was going over. There was the desperation in those words 'Help me' and then the acceptance of fate in the last sentence, and the thoughts for those left behind.

For a moment I couldn't read any more.

Then I found that there had been a survivor. One man, the mate, had been washed ashore in a lifeboat the previous day.

Was it possible then that my dad could also have survived the sinking of his trawler? But if so, why had he disappeared? Why did he wait all these years to come back into our lives?

I remembered there was a scrapbook of newspaper cuttings about a trawler disaster that my mum sometimes used to look through, but of course that was long gone. Everything went in the flood in 2007. Photographs, memories. All washed away. They say you don't know what you've got till it's gone. Well, that's true enough.

I moved back in with my mum and my nan just after the floods, never thinking it would be for so long. I thought I could help them stay afloat, pardon the pun, and I suppose I did. It was a council house, so we did what we could, but it took a while for the house to dry out and to get it redecorated. I heard of people whose insurance companies had paid for them to stay in caravans and hotels. Some had ended up better off than they were before, with everything new and fresh. But for most of us it wasn't like that. So much was lost.

Now there's just the two of us. My nan's eighty-seven and she's getting frail. I look after her, like she looked after us for so long. It's a short walk from the library to the home we share, the one where I was brought up.

* * *

I waited until Saturday afternoon, when my nan was sitting in her usual chair, nursing her cup of tea. Sometimes she would nod off, and I would have to dive across the room to retrieve her teacup before she spilt it into her lap. She always liked a cup and saucer, never a mug. Tray cloths, paper doilies, clean net curtains. She had a thing about keeping up standards, as if she aspired to a more genteel sort of lifestyle. Maybe that was why she had wanted my mum to do better for herself than marrying a trawler man.

"Nan, did you ever meet my dad?"

"No, pet. I didn't know anything about him, till his ship was lost. And then your mam was in such a state. Of course, they never found the crew, so there was no funeral. No proper chance to say goodbye. Mind, she couldn't have gone to funeral."

"Why not?"

"Well, that would've been just for the family, you know. He was married, you see, but I don't think he and his wife were getting on. Then your mam said she was in the family way. She couldn't even put his name on the birth certificate. Oh, I felt for her all right. Expecting a baby and no fella to support her. I said that flat of hers was no place to bring up a bairn. I said 'You come back home and live with us. We'll look after you both'. I didn't care what the neighbours said. If she wanted the baby, she should keep it. Well, your grandad had summat to say about it. But I said, 'It's not her fault her fella's not around.' Mebbe he'd have stood by her, mebbe he'd have done a runner. Well, we'll never know."

"So, he never knew he was going to be a dad?"

"No, his trawler went down and that was that. Of course, now they say all sorts about it. Spying on the

Russians, they say. But I don't know. Anyway, that was the end of that. You came along and we managed all right, me and you and your mam."

You always know when my nan has finished with a subject. She closes her eyes, as if to say, 'That's enough now.'

The story about a trawler spying on the Russians rang a bit of a bell with me. It was time to find out more.

* * *

On Monday I was back on the internet.

As soon as I searched for trawlers lost in 1974, one name kept appearing: the Gaul. I scrolled down the search results. The first one that caught my eye was from a BBC website 'On this Day':

No hope of survivors from missing Gaul trawler

So much for that then.

But Nan had said something about spying for the Russians. There was obviously more to the Gaul disaster than a simple sinking, however tragic. I settled down for a long read.

The Gaul sailed on January 22nd, 1974. On February 10th, she twice failed to report in. No trace of the ship was found or of its thirty-six crew, despite a search by British and Norwegian ships, helicopters and RAF aircraft. Unlike other trawlers that had been lost, there had been no mayday signal, no communication at all. Like the Titanic, it had been described as 'unsinkable', one of the new breed of factory ships with all the latest technology.

There were claims that the Gaul was involved in espionage. Had it been sunk by a Russian submarine? It was believed to have gone down in the Barents Sea off the coast of Norway. There were rumours that it had been seen spying on a military installation at Murmansk. Apparently, it wasn't unknown for trawlers to be used by the Navy for spying. The mystery surrounding its disappearance and the lack of a wreck fed rumours that crew members might still be alive.

What if my dad had survived and been taken prisoner? What if he had been living in Russia all this time? I read on.

The wreck was eventually found in 1997, eighty miles north of Norway, after a private search set up by a TV reporter, but the rumours and claims of a cover-up continued. Then, in 2002, the remains of four crew members were found and retrieved from the wreck. Where were the others? It all seemed to add to the speculation that there may have been survivors.

Two years later, the original enquiry into the loss of the ship was reopened, as a result of pressure from the families. No wonder Mum had kept all those newspaper cuttings. She must have been following the story all along. Yet she had never talked to me about it. I suppose she wasn't officially part of the group of grieving relatives and had got used to keeping things to herself. The enquiry concluded that the ship had sunk because two chutes had been left open, but the relatives didn't believe that such a basic mistake could have been made by the crew. The accusations of a cover-up failed to go away.

And that was that. So, did anyone survive? Could my dad still be alive? And who was he anyway?

I found the crew list. There was no one called Jim, but there were five called James. I didn't even know my dad's surname. I assume my mum did, but she couldn't put it on my birth certificate, could she? There was no proof, no blood test that could be done, no DNA testing in those days, and in any case, there was a wife.

I knew that Mum was born in 1946 and had me when she was twenty-eight. Was Jim older? There were several crewmembers with dates of birth in the 1940s, but only one called James. James Thompson was born in January 1942. I tried on the name for size: Helen Thompson. Sounded okay. Not that much different from Helen Johnson.

But could he have survived? If he had, where had he been? If there had been survivors, why was there nothing about it on the internet? And if no one had survived, why had that man claimed that he was my dad?

I tried to think about something else, but the questions kept swirling around in my head, like flood water.

A week later, the letter arrived.

CHAPTER FOUR

A Letter

Dear Helen

I don't blame you if you tear this letter up or throw it in the bin but please read it first. I know you were upset the other day and I would have been too if I'd been in your place. I shouldn't have sprung that on you about me being your dad but believe me it was as much a shock to me as it was to you.

I shouldn't have waited so long. I should have contacted your mam after I saw her photo in the paper, the one after the flood. I thought she'd be married, have kids and all that, but then I saw she was still Linda Jahnson, no mention of any family. And I just wanted to find something, to kind of find myself again. It's like I've been lost for years. It's too complicated to explain. But I didn't have the courage. I couldn't tell her what I'd done.

I never knew about you. I mean I didn't even know she'd had a baby. Honestly, believe me I had no idea. I didn't mean to leave her in the lurch. I hope you were all right. I mean both of you. I hope you've had a good life. I'm sorry I wasn't there, but I couldn't be. I couldn't come back.

The thing is I know what it's like growing up not knowing anything about your real parents. It happened to me too. Well I know it's different for you because you had your mam, but you must have wondered about your dad. I never knew my real mam and dad. The people that brought me up were great, they were my parents, and I know they did their best for me, or at any rate what they thought was best, but I always wondered if I should try and find my real mother. And then I sort of ceased to exist myself.

Anyway, I know this makes no sense. You probably never want to speak to me again, but if you want me to explain what happened, give me a ring. Or text me. I've put my number at the top. And if you don't, well I understand.

Jim (your Dad)

I read it and re-read it. It made no sense. If he was who he said he was, then where had he been all these years? What did he mean about being lost? What couldn't he tell Linda? Why did he say he couldn't have come back? Surely, he couldn't really be a survivor of the Gaul.

It was more likely that he wasn't. The chances were that he wasn't my dad. Maybe he was just someone else that Mum knew back then. Maybe they'd had a bit of a fling back in the day and he thought he might be my dad. Though Mum had never said there was anyone else. And they couldn't both have been called Jim, could they? But why would he pretend that was his name? And why had he changed it to something else? What did he even want from me?

I sent him a text.

I don't know who you are, but you're not my dad. I don't know what you want, but that's not my problem. Please don't contact me again.

Well, that was that. Except that it wasn't. There was something about him, something that I actually liked, something that seemed genuine and strangely familiar. He didn't seem like a weirdo or a stalker.

I would lie awake, turning it over in my mind. There was no one I could ask, no one who could tell me anything, no one who could answer my questions. Except him.

* * *

Two weeks passed. He'd been as good as his word and not contacted me again. In the end I had to do it. Against my better judgement, I sent the text.

I know I said I didn't want to speak to you again, but I think I need an explanation. Do you want to meet up for a coffee?

And that's how I found myself sitting in Costa Coffee, listening to the story of the man who said he was my father.

CHAPTER FIVE

Jim's Story

"I wasn't what you'd call a bright lad when I was at school. My mam and dad wanted me to stop on and do my exams, but I knew that wasn't for me. I had a mate who lived down Hessle Road. He had a bit of a swagger about him. He was a bit cocky, if you know what I mean. I used to walk down there with him, see the deckies in their fancy suits, and I wanted a piece of that, so I signed on as a galley lad. It was nineteen fifty-seven. My mam and dad were disappointed, but they weren't my real parents. I was adopted, you see. I found that out when I was fourteen and that's what decided me. 'You can't tell me what to do,' I said. 'You're not my real mam and dad'. I'm sorry I said that now, but it's too late to do anything about it. Now that I don't even exist.

"I didn't mind being a galley lad. It was my job to prepare the vegetables and wash up. There was a sack of spuds to peel for dinner and a sack for tea. Every dinner was meat and veg and every tea was fish. It was always a cooked breakfast as well. Mind, if the trip went on too long, it was fish for breakfast, dinner and tea. We had a mug of tea with our meals but if we wanted it at other times, we had to make our own, with our own tea. There was about twenty-four crew members altogether.

"If I got any spare time, I'd run up to see if anyone wanted their bunk or cabin tidying, to earn a few extra bob. Everyone else was given poundage, but not the galley boy.

"After that I was taken on as decky learner. I nearly got sacked for not making good enough tea for the skipper. If we took him tea, it was from our own tea stores. He used to tip it over the side if it was too strong. I found out later he had a stomach ulcer. Maybe that's why he was so bad-tempered. He used to watch us from the bridge and bawl at us if he saw anyone skylarking on deck.

"The day after we set off, we'd have a big party, but the next day, even if we had thick heads, we had to get everything prepared for the fishing. We went as far as Bear Island, Iceland, Greenland, even Newfoundland. We were usually out for about three weeks, though it depended on the markets. If they were good, we'd head back sooner.

"Sometimes we'd come back through the fjords. People pay a fortune to see them nowadays and we got paid for it!

"It wasn't a bad life really. And back in them days the fishing was good. We didn't like the engineers cos they did six hours on and six off, in the warmth, while we'd do eighteen hours on deck in the cold when we were bringing in the catch. In some of the boats the bunks would be in the bow and if the sea was rough, we couldn't get above for our meals.

"When we got back, we were straight off. Then the bobbers would come on board to offload the fish. They'd work from eight at night to eight in the morning to get the fish off. Next morning we'd come to office for the settling. Then off to Rayners. That was the pub we used to go in on Hessle Road. Home for a kip then we'd take the missus out for a meal and on to Baileys night club. Next day was for the rest of the family. Then we'd be off again. That's why they called us Three-Day Millionaires.

"I got married to Sandra when I was twenty-two. She was a bit of a bombshell if you know what I mean. But she had expensive tastes. First, she wanted a fridge and then a washing machine and then a colour TV and fitted carpets. None of my mates had anything like that, but she always wanted to be one better. And if we had a bad trip and there wasn't much money, she used to raise hell. Like it was my fault! She'd make me feel that small.

"We must have been married about ten years and things were getting really bad. She said it was my fault we didn't have any kids. Mind, I spent that much time sleeping on the settee, it's no wonder we didn't. We argued all the time about money. She'd want new carpets, new curtains. Nothing was ever good enough. I was never good enough. Truth to tell, I'd be happy to get back to sea.

"One day, I got back from Rayners and we had a massive row. I went back to pub and then off to Baileys with my mates. And that's where I met Linda. She was out with her friends too and we were all sat in a group, and we just got talking. It was like we'd known each other all our lives. I told her everything, stuff I'd never told anyone. About what it was like being married to Sandra. About being trapped with all the debts we'd got, for stuff we couldn't afford, stuff we'd bought on the never-never.

"I took her back to her place in a taxi. It was a flat that she shared with her friend, in one of those big houses down the Boulevard. She said she'd grown up on Hessle Road but then her family got a house on Northfield, and she'd moved back to the area. I spent the rest of the night there. I knew then that I had to leave Sandra.

"In the morning I had to sneak out before anyone saw me.

"I didn't know what to do. I couldn't face going home to Sandra. We were supposed to be going round to her mam's for Sunday dinner. I just walked round and round. I remember it was freezing cold. January. I don't know what it's like now round there, but it was getting pretty rough then. All them big houses were going to rack and ruin.

"Then I walked into town. I didn't really know where I was going. I just kept asking myself what I was doing with my life. Thirty-two years old and what was it all for? I didn't want to see anyone I knew, so I kept away from Hessle Road and headed for town-centre. I don't remember where I went. I know I had a few pints. I still had plenty of money in my pocket. I think I was in the George when I met him. Well, it was comical really. I saw him and he saw me, and we just started laughing. And everyone else joined in. The thing was we could have been brothers. Or twins. You know they say that everyone's got a doppelganger? Well, that was what it was like. I'd met my doppelganger. So, I bought him a drink and he bought me one, and so on.

"He said he was called Jack and he'd come from Grimsby. Like me, he was on trawlers, only he didn't get on with the skipper on his last ship, so he'd come to Hull. He was looking to get on a ship here and was taking a look round first. I told him I was going on a new ship next day and I said I'd show him round town. Like I said, I still had a bit of money in my pocket.

"I don't know what it was about him, maybe it was because we looked so alike. I never had a brother, and we had stuff in common. He didn't know his parents either. Only he'd grown up in a children's home. Then he'd got in with the wrong crowd. It sounded like he'd run wild for a time, got involved with a group of Teds, been in a spot of bother and moved around a bit.

"I don't remember much more about that day. I suppose we just carried on drinking.

"Next thing I knew I was waking up in some kind of alleyway, feeling like I'd done ten rounds with Mohammed Ali. I was stiff and bruised all over and I had a splitting headache. I had a vague memory of getting thrown out of some pub.

"I was in the old town, down one of the staithes off High Street that led down to the River Hull. I was lying on the cobbles and God knows what filth. It stank. And I was freezing cold. I had to get up and start walking just to get warm. It was middle of winter, remember. And then when I put my hand in my pocket, I realised my wallet was gone. And not just that, my ticket for ship. Well, it was too late now. The taxi would have come to my house early doors. You could go to jail if you didn't turn up on time.

"I didn't know what to do. I just started walking down High Street towards the fruit market. And then I was on Corporation Pier and the ferry was in. Lincoln Castle, I think it was. Funny that I remember the name. 'Lady of the Humber' they used to call her. That was before they built the Humber Bridge, though I think they'd maybe started on it back then. Going to Lincolnshire was like going to foreign parts!

"Well, I just got on. I don't really know what I was thinking – it was like I just needed to keep moving. I remember sitting in the waiting room at New Holland, keeping warm by the fire, and thinking where now? It was like I'd burnt my boats when I crossed river. And I remember thinking it was supposed to be my birthday. But it was like it didn't matter at all.

"I'd got just enough cash on me to catch train to Grimsby. Funny thing was, this lad on the train thought he recognised me. 'Now then, Jack,' he said.

"I told you we looked alike, didn't I? Anyway, once I'd convinced him that I wasn't Jack, we got talking and I found out a bit more about my new best mate of the day before. It turned out it wasn't just that he didn't get on with the skipper. Apparently, he'd been accused of stealing from one of the other men. It was never proved or taken to court, but he was blacklisted. I told this lad I was looking for work and he said they were wanting bobbers down at the dock.

"So that's what I did. I got myself taken on as a casual, so I didn't need any national insurance number. When they asked my name, I remember looking around and seeing the street name. Henderson Street. So, I called myself Steve Henderson, got digs in a Sally Army hostel in Brighowgate, and just lay low.

"You know Grimsby was the biggest fishing port in the world, back in the day. It was easy to disappear into the crowds.

"I reckoned that Jack had taken my ticket and my place on ship. You see it was my first trip on her so no one knew me, and I reckon he just got away with it. Of course, I'd told him all about myself, so he knew enough about me to blag it. And I reckon Sandra just thought I'd gone straight to ship.

"Then I heard the news. About the Gaul going missing with all hands. I couldn't believe it at first. She was like a real modern ship, one of them new factory ships. They said she was unsinkable. Like the Titanic. I saw the newspaper headlines and I read my name as one of the crew. What could I do? It was like the old me, Jim, didn't exist anymore. And suddenly I was free. Well, that's how it seemed to me. I just kept my head down, kept shtum.

"You might say it was cruel, but who was it cruel to? I'd long lost touch with the people who'd adopted me. That was right back in the fifties when I first went to sea. They thought I'd let them down. Well, maybe I had, but I reckoned they'd let me down. Anyway, that's in the past. I didn't have any kids. And Sandra? Well, I reckoned she'd be better off without me. She'd soon find herself another fella, someone who'd pay for her fancy clothes and stuff.

"Well, that's it really. I kept myself to myself. Did a bit of this and a bit of that. Nothing official of course. But I've always been handy and there's always people wanting stuff doing. Getting harder now. I'm not as young as I was. And I can't claim my pension when I don't exist. But I manage. I've got myself a little caravan by the sea.

"And then, a few years back I saw something in paper about the floods. There was a picture of Linda Johnson, aged sixty-one, and I knew it was her straight away. You see I'd often thought back to that night and imagined how it might've been different, if we'd met in different circumstances. It was like we were right for each other, in a way that me and Sandra never were. I even thought of writing to her, but I couldn't bring myself to say what had happened. She must have thought I'd gone down with the Gaul too. And that would've been the end of it for her. She'd have forgotten about me.

"But she was still called Linda Johnson. I remembered that was her surname because we were talking about names, me being a Thompson and her a Johnson. I'd asked her if her dad was called John. And she'd said that would make her a son not a daughter. The reason it stuck in my mind was that she'd said something about her dad being a bit of a nasty piece of work, and that's when I'd told her about being adopted. Anyway, I could tell from her surname in the paper that she hadn't got married or anything. And I kept thinking, maybe, just maybe, I could see her and tell her. Well, I never found the courage. But I kept the cutting from the paper.

"And then I decided it was now or never. I would come to Hull and look for her, I wouldn't even talk to her. Just see where she lived and maybe see her too. Just the once.

"But I was too late, wasn't I?

"I found Amber Close easy enough and I stood there for ages, but I didn't see anyone coming in or out. Then I asked this woman if Linda Johnson still lived down there, and she sort of looked at me a bit funny, and said, 'No, just her mam and Helen. Why are you looking for her?'

"I didn't know what to say. I just said, 'Oh I'm an old friend. Did Linda move out?'

"Then she looked at me funny again and said, 'Look if you want to talk to Helen, she works at library. It's just round the corner.'

"'Helen?' I asked.

"'Her daughter,' she said. 'I thought you said you were an old friend.'

"So that's how I found you. And I think I knew immediately. You were the spitting image of her."

24

CHAPTER SIX

The Floods

When he'd finished, I just sat there. I hadn't touched my coffee. I should have said something, but I couldn't. It was too much to take in. And he just sat there, looking kind of lost and frail.

Part of me wanted to take his hand, and part of me wanted to push him away. In the end, I said, "I'm sorry, I don't know what to say. I need to think about it." And I just left, leaving him sitting there, sort of small and shrunken, like my mum was, near the end of her life.

I knew about the newspaper article, the one with a picture of my mum. We kept it, as a memento. Well, as my nan said, we didn't have much else after the flood.

I remember the day of the flood so well, June 25th, 2007. And so does everyone else who lives round here.

You'd never have thought it was June. It was as if summer had been cancelled. It had been raining on and off, for days. For the last week, we'd had a bucket put out to catch water dripping through the ceiling of the library. Anyway, that particular day, a Monday I think, it was raining when I got up and it just didn't stop. It was cold as well.

I was living in a flat in the Old Town at the time. They'd converted one of the old warehouses by the River Hull into flats. It was great to be living so close to the city centre, able to go out for a drink with friends or to the Sugar Mill for a night out. I was single again after a relationship that had ended disastrously. But that's another story. Even though it was supposed to be summer, I remember putting on a coat because I knew I'd get drenched walking to the bus station.

The leak in the roof had got worse over the weekend and I was wishing we'd got something done about it. The last thing you need in a library is the water coming in. But it was a quiet morning. Then one of our regulars came in, an old chap who just came to read the papers and have a bit of company, I think.

"By 'eck, I thought I was going to be washed away out there," he said. "Pouring down the road like a river."

I put Radio Humberside on. It was true. The city was awash.

At that moment I got a call from Liz Walsh, the children's author who was scheduled to give a talk to children from our local school. She sounded distraught.

"I'm so sorry," she said. "Only I just can't get into Hull. Everyone's being turned back. Apparently, the roads are flooded."

"No worries." I was quite relieved really. The last thing we needed was a bunch of school kids dripping all over the floor. I tried ringing the school to tell them the workshop was cancelled, but I couldn't get through for nearly an hour. When I did, the school secretary spoke to me as if I was a fool.

"Well of course it's cancelled. We're just trying to get all the children picked up by their parents and taken home."

Then we got a phone call from Central Library. They told us we were best shutting up early and getting home while we could.

Oh well, I thought, an early finish today. I would go home and watch a video or something. Then I thought about Mum and Nan. They lived not far from the library, down one of the closes. I decided to call and check if they were okay. My mum hadn't been well recently, and she wasn't at work.

Outside the library doors, I was met by a huge puddle. I tried to skirt round it by walking over the grass, only to have my shoe sucked into the mud. I should have worn trainers (or wellies if I'd had any), not normal work shoes.

It was only a couple of streets to my nan's house, but it felt like a mile. As well as the driving rain, it was bitterly cold. And my feet were soaked. As soon as I turned into Amber Close, I realised how bad it was. Kids were splashing in the brown water. People were shouting from upstairs windows.

I rang mum on my mobile. I don't know why I hadn't before.

"No, don't you come round here," she said. "You get on home. I've got your nan upstairs with me and we're fine. I've just put the kettle on, and we've got the microwave in the bedroom, so we won't starve."

I remember the newspaper article. It said how my eighty-one-year-old nan was trapped in the house and couldn't get out to the doctor. There was a picture of her with my mum, both looking angry. All the décor was wrecked, and the council didn't seem bothered. "We lived through the blitz and now we've got this," a neighbour had said. The reporter commented that many former residents of Hessle Road, like Doris Johnson and her family, had moved to Northfields in the sixties and seventies. They were tough folk from the fishing community, but the estate hadn't lived up to their expectations. "We've had damp, we've had vandalism and now we've got floods."

All over the city, people were moved out of their houses. Some of them living in caravans, some staying with relatives. It was a year before many got back in their own homes. Some got swanky new kitchens and got their tatty old sofas and suchlike replaced with brand new ones. They were the winners, you could say. But others were the losers. For those in council houses, like my mum and my nan, they just had to stay put and wait for the house to dry out and get repaired. And it stank for ages.

I know. I moved back in with them to help them get it straight and so that I could contribute my bit to the household. Also, my mum was still not well.

It turned out she had cancer. That was the beginning of a long journey. Diagnosis and treatment and then remission. And then it started all over again. It went on for five years, hopes raised and then dashed. And then we lost her.

I wished my mum was here now, so I could ask her about Jim and that night they spent together.

My mum would know. She would know whether it was the same man. Even though he was in his seventies now, she would know. But she was gone, and it was just me and my nan now.

CHAPTER SEVEN

Exploring

I didn't say anything to my nan when I got in from meeting Jim. She was in her chair as usual. The TV was on, but I think she'd been asleep.

"Have you had a nice walk, pet? I'll come with you next time, when I'm feeling a bit more myself. Maybe in the spring."

It was late October, and I know she felt the cold more and more, even though the month had been mild and wet. She was always planning what she'd do when she felt a bit more herself, as if she could turn back time. As if the infirmities of age could somehow be reversed.

I put the kettle on and brought her another rug to put over her knees. She'd always been tiny, like a sparrow, but she seemed smaller than ever.

The next day was Sunday, so after I'd given Nan her breakfast and got her settled, I caught a bus into town. From the bus station, I walked past the shops on Jameson Street and King Edward Street to Victoria Square, then past the ruins of the Beverley Gate and down Whitefriargate, Silver Street and Scale Lane to the High Street. Being Sunday, the city centre was pretty quiet, and the cobbled streets of the old town were deserted. It was strange to think that this was once the most important street in the city, lined with merchants' houses, busy with river traffic in the days before the docks were built. Some of the old buildings had been regenerated, and a new pedestrian bridge over the River Hull linked the area with a modern hotel, but it must have been a gloomy sort of place in the 1970s. I wondered which of the narrow staithes leading down to the river was the one where Jim had woken up that January morning in 1974.

I joined a few families making their way along the High Street to the Museums Quarter. I've always worked closely with the museums because we're part of the same section of the city council, but I'd never visited the Arctic Corsair, the old trawler moored on the River Hull, behind the Streetlife museum. Even when I lived in my flat a stone's throw away from it, I'd never thought about visiting it. In my job I'd learnt a lot about the history of Hull. I knew all about Wilberforce House with its slavery museum, and the fact that William Wilberforce used to drink his ale in the Olde Black Boy opposite. When I was a child, the museums had all seemed rather dark and forbidding, located in a part of the town that was full of empty warehouses, far from the shops and department stores of the city centre. But in the last few years they had all been brightened up. I turned into the courtyard and entered the new shop and entrance area of the Hull and East Riding Museum. Tickets for the Arctic Corsair were free, like all the museums, but I needed to book onto a tour.

"While you're waiting, you can look at the exhibition next door."

A TV screen was showing a film about the fishing industry. I watched the rather grainy footage of a trawler being thrown about in the rough northern seas and of the ice that could form on the structure and cause it to capsize. I imagined my dad as one of those men in their oilskins. I remembered that message sent by the skipper of the Ross Cleveland 'We are going over'. What terror must my dad have felt as the Gaul capsized and sank?

But then, was it my dad? Or some imposter? This ne'er do well who took my dad's ticket and then drowned?

A small group of us boarded the Arctic Corsair. We descended the steep stepladder to the quarters below where the men slept and the hold where the fish were thrown. Our guide, an ex-trawlerman, showed us where the side net was hauled in and explained the difference between sidewinder trawlers like this and the stern trawlers which replaced them.

"Was the Gaul a stern trawler?" I asked.

"Aye, but it was a lot more modern than this," he said. "It was what they call a factory ship. Nearly brand new when it was lost."

I walked back along High Street, past the flats, where I'd enjoyed my bit of independence, and continued on through the underpass to the tidal barrage. It probably wouldn't have been there in 1974. Hull had changed a lot in my lifetime, with the regeneration of the old town. Once deserted warehouses were now trendy flats and nightclubs. What would it have been like in 1974, I wondered? The Deep certainly wouldn't have been there. It was hard to miss now, rising above the Humber like the prow of a titanic ship. Pulling up my collar against the chilly sea air, I followed the path round to the pier. I could smell fish and chips from the kiosk that was still open. Seagulls screamed overhead, no doubt hoping to swoop down for scraps. A few families were on the pier itself, some photographers trying to capture the iconic profile of the Deep. I tried to imagine what it was like when the ferry sailed from here, the one that Jim took to New Holland, before the Humber Bridge was built.

I decided to pop into the Minerva for a coffee to warm myself up. Perched on the edge of the Humber, it would have been here back in 1974, but what would it have been like then? Smoke-filled, no doubt. I sat in the tiny snug and looked at the photographs on the walls. It was impossible to escape from memories of the fishing industry if you were in Hull. Even the pavements were inlaid with metal sculptures of fish, forming a fish trail. There was one just outside the pub, on Minerva Terrace: a haddock. A couple of streets away was where they used to have the fruit market. I suppose that would have still been going strong in 1974, but it had closed now. The semi-derelict warehouses were being converted into artists' studios, and the whole area came to life whenever there were music festivals. In August the streets were jammed with revellers for the Humber Street Sesh, but it was pretty much deserted now.

Even the marina wouldn't have been there in 1974, I thought, as I walked back into town past the fancy pleasure boats that were moored there, jangling in the breeze. It was hard to imagine that it was once just a dock. I imagined my dad wandering the streets that cold January day. If he was my dad.

Still thinking about Jim and my mum, I took a bus to Hessle Road. It went up Anlaby Road, past blocks of flats that looked like they were built in the nineteen-sixties and then down Rawling Way to the roundabout where Hessle Road begins now. The facades of the shops and buildings looked like they dated back to Victorian times, but you only had to glance down the side streets to see that the terraces where my nan used to live had gone, replaced by modernish houses. I remember my nan talking about being rehomed to Northfield from the old, terraced houses: "They called them slums, and don't get me wrong, it was nice to have a proper bathroom and a garden and that when we moved, but they built some new slums here as well".

Eventually I reached the junction with the Boulevard, the long tree-lined avenue leading down to the fish dock. Jim said he'd spent the night here with my mum in her flat, the night I was conceived. I wondered which of the tall, yellow brick houses she'd lived in. I'd researched a bit about the street and found that the Victorian and Edwardian houses were originally built for wealthy fish merchants, but they'd fallen into disrepair during the seventies. It looked like their fortunes were being reversed now, to judge from the tidy railings and smart blinds, although some of them were obviously still multiple occupancy, if the rows of bins in the litter-strewn forecourts were anything to go by. The Hull School for Fishermen built in 1914 was still there, but I noticed it was now a school for schoolgirl mums. Well, at least Mum wasn't a schoolgirl when she got pregnant.

What would it have been like for my mum, I wondered, living her independent life, enjoying her job, her nights out with her mates, only to find that she was single and pregnant? What was it like for her going back to live with her mum, being shouted at by her dad? She must have been in her late twenties by then, hardly a teenager, but it was probably still difficult being an unmarried mother back then. Did she always know she'd keep the baby, the baby that turned out to be me? Was she never tempted to get rid of it? Of me?

I felt my thoughts moving into dangerous territory and hastily brought them back to 1974 and Linda, my mum, in her flat overlooking the lime trees that lined the Boulevard. What were her hopes and dreams before she moved back in with her mum and dad?

She'd told me once that she felt like she'd missed out on the swinging sixties, like they'd happened to someone else. Though she did see the Beatles when they performed at the ABC in Hull. She said she was about eighteen at the time, and they couldn't hear anything but the screaming.

It seems odd now that I'd never really asked her much about my dad, but I do remember asking her if she'd had any other boyfriends when she lived in her flat, and she'd just laughed. "I wasn't a nun, you know. Things were getting much freer by then, with the pill and everything. If only I'd been on it when I met Jim!"

"What? And not had me?" I'd asked. "Charming!"

Then she'd given me a hug and said of course she didn't regret having me. And that I was all she'd ever wanted, once I came along.

Did she really mean that? I wondered. Did she never imagine she might have met someone else? Or had an amazing career? I knew she'd been working in a bank when she got pregnant. She might have gone on to have a career in finance, and made something of her life, instead of being a single mum living on a council estate, still living with her own mum.

I laughed out loud. Unlike me, I thought. Because I'm just as free as a bird. No ties, no family, except for my nan, and, oh, living on a council estate and working in the local library.

She'd poo-pooed the idea when I suggested to her once that she could have had a good career. "Me? Working in finance? You must be joking. I never had the brains for it. Mind, I did all right at school, but I never stayed on. None of us did. It wasn't the thing. You just left and got a job. And then got married and had kids. I'd never have been a career woman. Though I was good with figures. My best subject at school was Maths."

So, was I what she would call a career woman? Unlike her, I'd stayed on at school, well, sixth-form college it was then. And carried on at the FE college and got a professional qualification. Maybe it was inevitable that I ended up as a librarian. Books were always my passion and still are. I guess I felt I could travel the world, travel through time, even travel inside other people's heads, just by reading books. It was easier than actual travelling, and less scary. Looking back, I wonder why I never wanted to move away from my hometown, but I think I was just happy to have a good job and to be independent. I could support myself, and I didn't need to depend on some man to come to my rescue.

Which was just as well. Because he didn't. Not when I might have needed rescuing.

CHAPTER EIGHT

My Story

It was when I was living in my flat that I met Alan. I'd left home and I was enjoying being able to see who I wanted, when I wanted. We met at the Sugar Mill – or was it still the Waterfront then? I can't remember. It seems strange to me now that a married man would be out clubbing, but he said that he and his wife took turns to have nights out with their mates. Now that I'd heard Jim's story, I found myself thinking about that night he'd met my mum in Baileys, him a married man, her a young woman living in a flat. But our stories turned out very differently.

It began with a dance, and then a drink, and then he walked me the short distance back to my flat. I invited him in, and so it began. As far as I was concerned, he was the only one who was doing anything wrong. It would have been different, I suppose, if I'd known his wife, but I didn't. And I enjoyed our little affair. It made me feel like a character in a book. Also, some relationships can turn a bit flat after a while, I imagine, when you begin to take each other for granted or you start having petty squabbles over who does the washing up, but we kept the magic.

When I was at work, doing some routine filing, I would feel a shiver of anticipation at the prospect of seeing him later that evening. I could spend time getting ready and setting the scene.

My flatmate, Amy, didn't ask too many questions. I suspect she knew what was going on, but I guess she thought it was none of her business. It must have been around that time that she started seeing Richard, who she would go on to marry, so I guess she was preoccupied with her own love life.

So, everything was fine, up to a point. The relationship suited both of us. I always seem to choose men that are either unsuitable or unavailable. Was it my way of making sure that I didn't get too committed, or tied down, as I saw it? The pattern began with my first boyfriend, back in sixth form. He left to go to university at the other end of the country, as I knew he would, while I stayed in Hull. After that there were holiday romances, as well as men that were about to leave the country and not return, or in Alan's case, were already married. Maybe it was my way of avoiding disappointment. If I chose someone that was unable to commit, I wouldn't have to feel so let down if they didn't stick around. Was I making a deliberate choice or a subconscious one? I don't know.

It was of course the usual story with Alan: my wife doesn't understand me, our marriage is on the rocks, I'll get a divorce when the time is right. But I never really believed it. Or cared. I enjoyed his company and the time we spent together, without having to worry about whether it was forever. He was outrageously good-looking, I thought, and I was flattered that he was willing to risk so much to be with me. Also, I liked the fact that there were no strings. I didn't want to fit the stereotype of the Other Woman, the one that eventually is discarded instead of the wife. But I didn't feel guilty either. I'd never met his wife, or children, and had no wish to. It was none of my business. If he chose to have some fun on the side, then why not? And it was fun. For a while.

The fun had to be kept private of course. It was an indoor relationship, mainly conducted within the four walls of my flat, to be honest. Or in quiet, out of the way pubs, where we wouldn't meet anyone he knew. But mainly in my flat, or more precisely in my bed.

He would visit at odd times, whenever he could get away, he said. And I rather enjoyed the cloak and dagger stuff. Maybe it added a bit of spice to the liaison. But if I look back now, I think of closed doors, closed curtains, keeping the sun out.

Then, bizarrely, I got pregnant. Not so bizarre really, considering I was in my late twenties and having sex. It was just a blip with contraception. Well, getting pregnant was never part of the deal in our relationship. I knew he wouldn't want the complication of another child, outside his marriage. And I didn't want it either. So, I didn't tell him. I just did what had to be done. And that was that.

Only, that was also the end of our relationship, the End of the Affair, you might say. The fact that I didn't want to tell him showed how shallow it all was. Meaningless really. What was the point? And if I did want a baby, at some point, there was still time, if the right person came along.

But they didn't, and when I was thirty-three, I moved back in with mum and my nan, and that really was that.

Where had the last six years gone since I moved back in with them? First there was the house to get sorted after

38

the flood. Then there was mum to look after when she was really ill. And now my nan, who was getting on for ninety. Somehow, I'd got used to being part of an all-female household again, just like when I was growing up. I couldn't imagine how a man would fit into that.

I thought about Jim and what he'd told me about his unhappy marriage, how he'd just put up with it until he had the chance to escape. He didn't know he was a father. I suppose he had no reason to assume he was, even after he saw Mum's photograph in the paper. The article never mentioned me.

But if what he said was true, I had a father. And what did that mean? I'd never known what that was. What did it mean to me that I now had a living parent? What did it mean to him to have a daughter?

I wondered if I should tell my nan. What would she say? Would she tell me to see Jim again? Or to forget him? She never had a kind word to say about men. Should I just perhaps raise the possibility that my dad might still be alive and see how she reacted?

CHAPTER NINE

Nan's Story

"Nan", I said, "what if my dad wasn't on that trawler that sank? What if he'd just done a runner?"

"Aye well, he wouldn't be the first. Makes no difference now though, does it? We managed, me and your mam. Well, your grandad was here too, at first, not that he was much help. He was always drunk. And he didn't think we should have had your mam back home. 'Throw her on the streets. That's what they did in my day'. Well, that was true enough, but it wasn't happening to any daughter of mine, I can tell you."

I went over and kissed her cheek.

"I said if he didn't like it, he could sling his hook. Which he did, after a fashion. Fell down the stairs one night when he was drunk. When you were still a baby."

"What? When he was at sea?" I pictured those steep steps on the Arctic Corsair.

"No love. Not when he was out at sea. They weren't allowed to drink much at sea, not once they started fishing. That's why they went mad when they came ashore. Oh no, it was when he was at home. Well, good riddance I say."

"Nan! How can you say that? You were married to him. Didn't you love him?"

"No, not really. Not when I got to know him. And he never loved me. Never forgave me that he wasn't my first."

"What? You never told me that, Nan. I thought everyone was a goody-goody in your day."

"Oh, you'd be surprised at what went on. Well, it was the war you know."

"What was it like, Nan, in the war?"

"Well, we just got on with it, didn't we?"

"I know you did, Nan, but tell me. What about the bombs?"

"Let me see. Now at first, when the bombing began, we used to go down to the air-raid shelter. You know, we all had one at the end of the garden. If you had a garden, that was. Well, we did, because we lived in Hessle back then. It was only a little garden, not much more than a yard really, but there was room to grow a few cabbages and suchlike. Well, we all had to, didn't we, in the war. But I never liked it in the shelter. It was horrible and musty and full of spiders. So, after a bit, we used to stay in the house when the air raid warning sounded. We used to go in the cupboard under the stairs. It was a bit of a squash, if we were all there, but we hardly ever were. My dad was a warden you see, and my mam drove ambulances."

"Doesn't sound very safe," I said. "You must've been terrified, all by yourself."

"Well, I wasn't usually by myself. If my friends were round, it was a bit like playing sardines. The thing was, after the raids were over, you'd see houses that were hit, but the stairs were still there, so that's why we sheltered under them. There were big public shelters too, but one of them got hit. Some people left the city at night and slept in the fields. Others just sat under their dining tables because it got to be so regular. It was terrible really. You never hear about it, all the people that got killed. Hundreds of them. You wouldn't believe it. All the big shops were hit in town centre. Hammonds, Thornton Varley, Edwin Davis."

I thought I remembered my mum talking about some of those shops. "Did any of the bombs land near you, Nan?"

"I remember them dropping mines on Gipsyville. I wanted to live there when we got married. There were nice council houses with gardens, but it wasn't easy getting somewhere after the war, with so many houses getting bombed. You won't remember it. Bomb sites everywhere. There was one at the end of our street. That was when we lived off Hessle Road. Your grandad wanted to be nearer to docks. There were no gardens. Just a yard at the back to hang out your washing. No bathroom. No indoor toilet. But we didn't know any different. It was all right. Your neighbours would do anything for you. Not like here. You never locked your door. Well, there was nothing to steal. My mam and dad didn't like it. They said I'd come down in the world, marrying a fisherman, living on Hessle Road. But it wasn't all bad. We moved a few times, but always stayed in the same area. Then we moved here, and it wasn't so good. I was stuck with your grandad. I thought he might give up on the drinking, but it was worse. And it wasn't like he'd be just round the corner. He had to get a taxi home. I never knew when he'd be back. And after your mam moved out, well it was just me and him. Anyhow I managed. And then when your mam moved back in, I was scared he'd take it out on her as well."

"You said my grandad wasn't your first. Did you have a boyfriend before then? What happened? Did your mum and dad think he was better than my grandad?" I thought about it. Funny she'd never told me any of this before, although she liked talking about when she was a child, more and more these days. It seemed as if her distant memories were becoming more and more vivid as she faded physically. Then I thought about it. "Did he get killed in the war?"

"No pet. He didn't. At least I don't think so. I don't really know what happened to him. And my mam and dad never met him."

"So, what happened?"

"My mam and dad weren't around much. Like I said, my dad was a warden, you know, in the ARP, and Mam was out driving ambulances, so they just left me to get on with it. I was old enough to look after myself. Well, I thought I was. I was only about fifteen when I think about it."

"Didn't you worry about what might happen to you? I just can't imagine what it was like."

"You know I found it quite exciting, really. I know that sounds bad now that I say it. But we lived in Hessle then, and most of the bombs were in Hull, near the docks or along Hessle Road, and anyway I had my friends for company. And not just my friends."

"Your boyfriend?"

"We were what we'd call sweethearts, for a while anyway. He was in the Merchant Navy, home on leave. Anyway, one thing led to another, and I didn't know

43

much about what we called the facts of life, back then, and there it was. Bun in the oven, we used to call it."

"What? You got pregnant, Nan? Did you tell him? What did he say?"

"Oh, he was back on his ship by then. I wrote, but he never replied."

"What did your mum and dad say?"

"They wouldn't speak to me at first, when they found out. Then they said that no one needed to know. I could go away."

"What do you mean?"

"There was a mother and baby home. It wasn't far away. I went to stay there as soon as I couldn't hide it anymore. They said I'd been evacuated to Goole to stay with your Auntie Elsie. The bombing was really bad by then. I was due in February, but I was early. It was so cold, terribly cold. I remember it now, the cold…"

My nan closed her eyes as her voice trailed off.

"Nan? What happened to your baby?"

"What? Oh, it was a long time ago. We don't need to go into that now. What's done is done, as they say."

"So, you never told anyone?"

"No. Not till I married your grandad. I told him on our wedding night. Had to, you see. He would've found out sooner or later. But he wasn't happy about it, I can tell you. Told me never to speak of it again. I think that's why he was always so hard on me."

"How old were you when you got married, Nan?"

"I was twenty-one."

"And did you love him then?"

"Well, he was a bit of a catch back then. Everyone loved him. You know, larger than life. Always up for a good time. Of course, he changed. He always liked a drink, but it took over, really. Like I said, he was on the trawlers then, and he couldn't drink so much when he was at sea, so he'd make up for it when he got home. Then he'd take it out on me."

"Why did you put up with it, Nan? Why didn't you just leave him?"

"Well, he said I deserved it. Damaged goods, he called me. He said no one else would want me. That's what my mam and dad had said too. But anyway, we had Linda, your mam, and that was all I wanted."

I was about to ask her again about the baby she'd had during the war, but something told me the subject was closed.

Outside I could hear the wind rising.

CHAPTER TEN

What the Storm Blew in

The subject may have been closed for my nan, but not for me. What happened to her baby?

The next morning, it was a struggle to walk to work. All weekend they'd been predicting that St Jude's storm was about to hit the UK. There were dark rumours that it would be as bad as the great storm of 1987. In the event, it mainly hit the south, but there were still branches blown down from trees.

As soon as I got the chance, I logged on and tried to find out what happened to unmarried mothers in Hull during the war.

I soon discovered that there was a mother and baby home called Hope House. Did it really provide hope for the young women who ended up there?

It opened in 1811 on Wincolmlee, that narrow back street that winds through warehouses alongside the River Hull, and it was originally called the Hull Female Penitentiary. The name made me shudder. It created an image in my mind of female penitents, clothed in sackcloth and ashes, repenting for the sin of getting pregnant. Apparently, it was set up to rescue 'fallen girls'.

Is that what my nan was? And my mum? I suppose Nan rescued her. Who would have rescued me if I'd gone ahead and had the baby? Would I have needed rescuing?

I pulled my thoughts back from that direction and carried on reading.

The institution closed in 1825 but then reopened in 1837 on Anlaby Road in Hull. It now took in girls from the East Riding and Lincolnshire, as well as from the city itself. My nan had said that her family lived at Hessle, to the west of Hull, just inside the East Riding. I read that the girls usually stayed for three months, six weeks before the birth and six weeks after. When I tried to imagine all those girls in Victorian times, I had a picture in my head. They'd be wearing long brown dresses with white aprons, sweeping floors and peeling potatoes. But it must have been different, I supposed, when my nan got pregnant. Was that where she'd gone?

It turned out to be a red herring. Hope House closed in 1937, before the war had even started. But she had definitely said that she went to a mother and baby home, so where was it?

I found accounts of life in some of these homes from other towns and cities in the nineteen-fifties, so were there similar ones in Hull after Hope House closed?

I was so engrossed that I was quite oblivious to my immediate surroundings. It was only when I heard someone clearing his throat in a rather purposeful manner that I became aware that I had a customer.

"Sorry to disturb you. I can see you're busy. Just wondered if you could spare me a moment."

"Yes, yes, of course. How can I help?" I felt my face turning bright pink. I'd been caught in the act of doing my own research instead of focusing on my work. But it wasn't just that. Was it the way he spoke? Definitely not local, though I couldn't quite place his accent. Or was it the way his grey-blue eyes crinkled at the corners when he smiled?

"I just wondered if you had anything in your local history section about Tolkien and his time in East Yorkshire. I know I'd be better going to Central Library, but I happened to find myself here. Long story. No, I can see it was a daft idea. Sorry to bother you."

And with that he turned away, no doubt as a result of my gormless expression. Tolkien? East Yorkshire? What?

"No, wait," I said, playing for time. "Let me have a look. Erm… Tolkien…. I'm sure we'll have something." Actually, I doubted it very much. We had a tiny local history section, but I just needed to not let him get away. "Erm…did you say he spent time in East Yorkshire?"

"Yes, during World War One. Don't worry. I was only asking on the off chance. Thing is I'm just waiting for someone. Is there anywhere I can get a coffee near here?"

He was going to get away! I thought quickly. "Look, I'll tell you what, I was just about to make myself a coffee. Why don't you take a seat and I'll bring one for you?"

"Oh no, I couldn't possibly." I was willing him to agree. "Well, if you're sure it's no bother…"

No bother? I must have fairly skipped to the kitchen. It's not really a kitchen, more of a cupboard. But it's got a kettle, a tiny fridge and a sink. And a bit of privacy where I could let a silly grin appear on my face. Which mug to give him? The grimy one with 'Keep calm and read a book' or the clean one with my name on it? No, that would be too weird. I hastily scrubbed at the other one to remove the brown ring round its base. Did he take sugar? Milk? Why was I feeling all dithery? What was the matter with me?

He was already sitting in the comfy seating area when I came out with the coffees. Where should I put myself? Not next to him. Too intimate. Not opposite, too direct. I couldn't let him see me blushing. I took a seat at right angles to him.

"So, you're waiting for someone?" I asked.

"Yes, you see I'm a bit of an idiot. I've managed to lock my keys in the boot of the car, so I'm waiting for someone to bring me the spare set."

"Your wife?" I asked, too obviously, as my face turned even hotter.

He laughed, and I thought again how nicely his eyes crinkled at the corners. "No. It's my lodger, Dan. We have this weird car-share thing. Sorry, I should have introduced myself. I'm Neil."

Was he gay? "I'm Helen."

"Yes, I know, The name badge. And the mug."

It was my turn to laugh. In a high-pitched girly way. What was the matter with me? Well, I knew. I'd been there before. But not since Alan, not for ages.

It turned out that he was on his way into Hull and had decided to cut through the estate, which he didn't really know. After going over an unexpected speed bump, he'd heard something rattling in the back.

"It's one of those weird cars where you have to unlock the boot separately. I must've put the keys down when I was investigating the noise and then locked them in when I shut the boot. Rooky error really. You can see cars aren't really my thing. I usually cycle."

"They're not my thing either. I don't even have a car. At least you can drive."

"That's not what Dan says. He says I drive like a girl. His words, not mine. I don't think girls can't drive. That's just what he's like. He thinks the car's wasted on me. But then he knows I'm not likely to smash it up by driving like a speed-freak. To be fair, I'm just not really into cars. You know, the whole green thing."

"The green thing? Oh, the environment. Yes, of course. So, Dan's your lodger. How's he going to get here if you've got his car?"

"He's going to use my bike."

"No, really? A pushbike? He's not going to be very happy, is he?"

"Oh, he'll get over it. He owes me anyway."

"What for?" Was I asking too many questions?

"For putting him up. Putting up with him. Giving him somewhere to sleep. Putting up with all his stuff in my house."

It turned out that Neil had offered Dan a room when he had nowhere else to stay after his marriage broke up. From what he told me, Dan was a bit of a womaniser, so it was no wonder his marriage had ended.

"And before that? Have you always lived alone?" There I was again, asking too many questions, but he didn't seem to mind.

"On and off," he laughed.

"Never found the right person? Me neither." Oh no, I was definitely being too obvious. I thought I'd better change the subject. "So, tell me about this Tolkien thing."

His eyes lit up. It was obviously his passion.

"So, I discovered that Tolkien actually stayed near Hull during the First World War. He was even treated in a Hull hospital. I was on my way to Central Library, actually, to do some research. And then when I had the silly incident with the car, I spotted this place and thought I'd just ask, on the off chance."

Now that I didn't feel on the cusp of him walking away and disappearing for ever, I was able to admit that we didn't really have much of a local history section. "What you really want to do is visit the History Centre, though. They've got a local studies section. Do you know where it is?"

He admitted that he wasn't sure. Having only lived in Hull for a couple of years, he was still finding his way around.

"I've got a friend who works there. Amy. I'm sure she'll help you out. I could give her a ring. When do you think you'll be going?"

"Well. probably not today, now. It'll have to be this week, though, while it's half-term."

"Oh, you're a teacher?" Of course he was.

"Afraid so. But I might get the bus next time, or cycle. Leave the babe-magnet for Dan."

"The what?"

"Oh, he calls the car his babe-magnet, because it's a convertible, even though it's as old as the hills. It seems to work for him, though. I wish it didn't. I wouldn't mind being able to walk round my own house without having to bump into his er… guests." There was a ring tone from his pocket. "That'll be him now with the keys. Best be off. Thanks for the coffee."

"You're welcome. Bye!" Would I ever see him again?

"Bye, Helen. Oh, and can I give you a ring?"

What?

"About the Tolkien thing."

After he left, I spend the rest of the day in a sort of daze. I put books back on the shelves, and then realised I'd lost all notion of alphabetical order. And as for the Dewey system: what was that about? I was behaving like a love-sick schoolgirl. What school did he teach at? Why didn't I ask him?

All thoughts of family history had gone out of my head.

I wondered if I should take another look at Tolkien. I'd read the books years ago and seen the film of the Lord of the Rings, but fantasy wasn't really my thing. I liked the idea of going on a journey, but I'd rather read about travelling to real places. Actual travelling just hadn't been a part of my life. People I knew went on holiday to Spain and Turkey and suchlike, but it was all about the sun and the sea and the hotels. Even when I was a student, it never occurred to me to have a gap year or go travelling. There was never any money anyway, and who would I go with? In books, I could go anywhere I wanted.

My other problem with reading fantasy was that I liked to read books with characters that I could identify with. I could imagine I was Jo March in *Little Women*, Elizabeth Bennet in *Pride and Prejudice*, Jane in *Jane Eyre*. Another of my favourite heroines was Lucy Snowe in *Villette*. Like Jane, she falls for someone apparently out of reach, but I loved the way Charlotte Bronte left the ending ambiguous. It felt like real life, a bit ragged, not all neatly sewn up with a Happy Ever After. Most of Tolkien's characters, on the other hand, were male, and I couldn't really identify with a hobbit.

A quick search in the sci-fi and fantasy section produced a copy of *The Lord of the Rings*. Flicking through its hundreds of pages, I remembered that there was one character who had come alive for me: Eowyn, the young lady-warrior who falls hopelessly in love with Aragorn, the heir of kings. I pictured him in the film with his long straggly hair and piercing blue eyes. It was hopeless because he has already given his heart to Arwen Evenstar, the beautiful and noble half-elf. How frustrating to really fall for the one person you can't have. Another man that was unavailable. And unsuitable, because he was apparently about ninety, despite his good looks.

CHAPTER ELEVEN

An Excursion

Every time the phone rang that week, I would feel a delicious shudder of anticipation, followed by a thump of disappointment. Then I would give myself a mental dressing-down for being besotted with someone I'd only met for half an hour. Had I only imagined that there was some chemistry between us?

When he did ring, it was just before I left work on the Friday and had given up all hope. He asked me if I fancied a trip out the next day.

"What? In the babe-magnet?" I asked.

He told me he was planning a drive into Holderness to visit some of the places where Tolkien was supposed to have stayed. It was an unexpected invitation, but why not?

"I'm working in the morning, but I finish at one," I replied.

"Right, one o'clock it is. I'll pick you up from work."

My nan noticed when I brought her morning cup of tea. "You're looking nice, love. Doing something special?"

I just planted a kiss on her downy cheek and laughed. "You never know!"

"Well, take care love."

The red car was indeed a sporty little number and completely mis-matched to Neil, with his hiking boots and scruffy jacket.

"Are we going to be doing a lot of walking?" I asked.

"Why? No, not really. Oh, I always dress like this. When I'm not at work. Dan says it's no wonder I never pull." He grimaced.

I suppose I could have said he'd pulled the moment he walked into the library, but I didn't. We carried on chatting as we drove east out of Hull and into the countryside. The conversation came easily. We were heading for a place called Thirtle Bridge. He pointed it out on the map that he'd passed to me.

"Watch the road!" I yelped, as he veered onto the grass verge.

"Sorry, yes. Not really used to driving, especially something as powerful as this."

The way he drove, you'd never have known it was a powerful car. He sort of trundled along, absent-mindedly, seeming to care nothing about all the cars that overtook him on the winding country roads.

He stopped suddenly. "Right, this is it!"

"This is what?" There was nothing but brown ploughed fields stretching to the horizon in every direction.

"So, this is where Tolkien was stationed during World War One."

"What? In a field?"

"There was a camp here."

I had to admit to feeling a little underwhelmed, but I liked Neil's enthusiasm.

"What got you so interested?" I asked. "Is Tolkien your specialist subject or something?"

He laughed. "I'm not preparing to go on Mastermind, if that's what you mean. No, my subject's Geography really. That's what I teach anyway. But I've always had a thing about Tolkien's books. Ever since I was old enough to read them. I was one of those children that's always reading. Or out wandering the countryside."

"Me too," I said. "Well, more the books than the countryside. Were you an only child too?"

"Yes, I was born when my parents were getting on a bit. I don't think they really knew what to do with children, so they just left me to myself."

"And now?"

"Well, I still enjoy my own company. I'm happiest reading, or walking. I think that's what got me into Geography, walking by the sea in Norfolk, thinking about how the land's been shaped by the weather and the tides. And then I started thinking about the environment and everything that could change or be lost, if we don't change what we do."

I looked over the endless expanse of fields, with hardly a tree or hedgerow to be seen.

"Okay, I admit there's not much to see here," he said. "Do you fancy fish and chips?"

We drove on to Withernsea, where we parked near the cliffs and descended several flights of steps to the beach. A stiff breeze was blowing my hair over my face, and I wished I'd been wearing more substantial footwear as we clambered over the wooden breakwaters that ran from the seawall to the sea. I struggled to catch up with Neil who was striding on ahead. As I watched him, I felt a pang of something I hadn't felt for a long time.

Once we reached the town, we bought our fish and chips and sat on a bench looking out to sea. The sun was already low, and the waves were edged with silver. Behind the pier towers the sky had touches of pink and lilac. I edged closer to Neil, longing for him to put his arm round me, but he was looking up at the sky. His grey-blue eyes were like reflections of the North Sea.

"Greylag geese," he said, indicating a v-formation flying overhead.

"You like birds then?" How lame a question was that?

"You should come to Spurn one day. That's where you need to go to see birds."

"Yes, I'd like to." Had it been an invitation, or just a suggestion?

As the temperature dropped, I shivered.

"Here, take this," he said removing his jacket.

"What about you?"

"Oh, I never notice the cold," he replied, "but we'd best be getting back. I'm guessing Dan will be needing the car."

His down-filled jacket felt like a hug. I inhaled its scent. It smelt of the ploughed earth and salty sea-air.

CHAPTER TWELVE

Into the Woods

After that I didn't see him for a while. He was back at work, and although we'd exchanged mobile phone numbers, there'd been no particular commitment to stay in touch or to meet again. I'd sent him a text:

Lovely day yesterday. Thanks xx

He replied:

Sorry about Thirtle Bridge. Nice fish and chips though xx

Nothing about meeting up again. Two kisses were good though. But only reciprocating the two I'd sent. Maybe I could find another pretext to text him again. Perhaps I could find something out about Tolkien? Or spot a rare bird?

"Did you have a nice time with your young man?" asked Nan.

"He's not my young man. We're just friends." Is that what we were?

"And are you seeing your friend again?"

"I don't know."

* * *

It was a couple of weeks later when I got another text from him:

Do you fancy another trip out on Saturday afternoon? xx

I felt my stomach do that lurching thing. Thank God, he couldn't see me dancing round the room.

This time, I was prepared with a coat and boots. As I slipped into the passenger seat, he gave me that smile. "I'm glad you could come."

"Where are we off to today then?" I tried to sound casual, but I couldn't stop smiling too.

We were heading into Holderness again, but this time we drove into a village. He pulled up at the side of the road, near an inviting-looking pub.

"Not fish and chips today then?"

"No, we're heading for the woods." He strode on with that long loping walk and I walked quickly to keep up. The metalled road gradually became gravelled and then narrowed to a path, deep in fallen leaves and crunching with conkers. I was glad I'd worn my boots this time. To our right was a small wood and then a churchyard. Next to the kissing gate that led to the church, a well-worn path led into the trees.

"You have to imagine it in the spring," he said. "It's Tolkien's hemlock glade. Though I don't think it would have been hemlock, more likely to be cow parsley."

I looked at him blankly. I mean I've read *The Hobbit* and *The Lord of the Rings* (and seen the films) but I'm not quite the Tolkien expert that Neil seemed to be.

"So, when Tolkien was stationed at Thirtle Bridge in 1917, his wife stayed here in the village, and one day she danced for him in the woods."

"What? Naked?"

"I didn't say naked."

"Oh no, you didn't. It would be a bit chilly though."

"It was the spring. But the thing is that he then went on to write the story of Beren and Luthien, where a mortal man falls in love with an elf woman after seeing her dancing in the woods. And that story comes up again in *The Lord of the Rings* when Aragorn falls in love with Arwen."

Okay, if anyone else had said that, I would have written them off as the sort of nerd that spends too much time in their room playing fantasy computer games. But Neil wasn't like that. I could tell that he was seriously moved by all this stuff. I liked his intensity and passion. Well, passion for something at any rate, but I wasn't sure it was passion that he felt for me. There was definitely a chemistry between us, at least I think there was, but he didn't seem interested in taking things any further.

Later, over a pub lunch, I tried to bring the subject round to more personal matters. He was telling me more about the story of Beren and Luthien.

"Have you ever been in love?" I asked. "I mean, really in love, so that you would follow them to the ends of the earth just to be together?"

"Not for a while," he said. "And I'm not sure it was love."

"What happened? Sorry, I don't mean to pry, if you'd rather not talk about it."

"She wanted children. And I didn't. And that was the end of that." Not gay then, so that was a start.

"Why didn't you?"

"I just don't think I could bring a child into this world, the way it is."

"And do you still think that?"

"Why would I change my mind?"

For some reason, I felt the urge to argue. "But what about Tolkien? What if he'd felt like that? I mean he lived through two wars. He must have felt that the world was a terrible place to bring a child into, but it didn't stop him." I was pretty sure that Tolkien had fathered children.

"But that was before we knew what the human race was doing to the planet."

I couldn't really answer that, but I wanted to carry on arguing, as if it was my job to defend the right of every unborn child to exist. And why? Hadn't I turned down the one real chance I'd had to be a mother? I felt tears spring to my eyes, whether of anger or self-pity, I didn't know. It wasn't even as if we were in a relationship. Yet it felt as if he was closing that particular door for me for ever.

We were both quiet on the way back to Hull. I was afraid that I'd wrecked what we had, whatever that was. Yet somehow when we got to the end of our road, I didn't want to let him go. I think I was afraid that if I did, I wouldn't see him again. And I wanted to.

"Come and meet my nan," I surprised myself by saying.

Nan was of course delighted to meet him. She fussed around, insisting that she would make him a cup of tea and that he sat in the best chair. She even produced a tray with a napkin on it and a plate of biscuits.

I could tell that she liked him. After he'd left, she wouldn't stop talking about what a nice young man he was, how well-spoken and polite. "Though I think he could smarten himself up a bit. What he needs is someone to take care of him, I expect. A teacher, did he say? Now there's a good job. You could have been a teacher. You always liked books and reading. I said you're never going to meet anyone if you work in a library."

I was about to point out that I had actually met Neil whilst working in a library, but realised I'd fallen into Nan's trap of talking about him as if he was my boyfriend.

"He's not my boyfriend, Nan," I said.

"But you wish he was, don't you?" she asked mischievously.

She was right, of course. Even though he never wanted children and even though he was obsessed with Tolkien and the environment and birds, I wished he'd put his arms round me in that wood and kissed me.

"I don't know if I'll be seeing him again," I said.

"Oh, get along with you. I saw the way you were looking at him."

Oh dear, was I really that obvious?

CHAPTER THIRTEEN

The End of the World

She was right, of course. I did see him again.

"Nothing Tolkien-related this time," he said. "How would you like to go to Spurn?"

I misheard him. "Spain? Really?"

"No, Spurn. Spurn point. The end of the world, as we know it. Well, the end of Holderness, anyway. Have you ever been?"

I hadn't, and to be honest it wouldn't have been my first choice for a November outing. But to go anywhere, with him… I hadn't been able to stop thinking about him. This time, I decided, I would make a move, even if he didn't, and see what happened.

The opportunity arose as we were walking down the narrow road that runs along the peninsula, separating the Humber estuary from the North Sea. To our right, the wide river opened out beyond the mudflats. Birds with long narrow beaks were foraging in the mud. Neil told me what they were, but I've forgotten. Every so often, he would stop and look through his binoculars at something dabbling in the mud or skimming over the water. To our left rose the sand dunes that separated the road from the beach. The road itself was uneven and criss-crossed by railway tracks that disappeared into nothing. Sometimes it would take a sudden change of direction.

"It's where the peninsula's moved. They've had to keep rerouting the road," he explained. "You see how it's broken up into sections so that it can be re-laid. But they can't keep on fighting the forces of nature."

I was feeling the forces of nature myself. It was cold and we were walking side by side, so close that our sleeves were brushing against each other. I slipped my arm into his and snuggled up closer. I could pretend it was just for the warmth. I was no longer even listening to what he was saying. Then he took my hand, squeezed it, and kept hold of it. We stayed like that as we walked towards the lighthouse, talking of this and that, but my mind and all my consciousness focussed on him and our proximity and the current flowing through our hands.

Suddenly he stopped. "Look," he said, pointing across the mudflats.

I couldn't see anything. He passed me his binoculars and put his arm round my shoulder to guide me into looking in the right direction. Then I saw it, a large white bird. "What is it?" I asked.

"It's an egret. They'd become very rare, but they're starting to come back."

I've never really been into birdwatching, but I could have stayed there forever, nestling into his chest, his arm round me, his hand over mine, holding the binoculars. I turned to look at him, and we kissed for the first time. He tasted as I imagined he would, of the sea and the earth and the shoreline and the cool November air.

Then he jumped up. "Come on," he said. "We don't want to risk getting stranded. One more high tide and this could become an island. Let's go back along the beach."

And he was off. I followed him up the sandy path that led between the clumps of dune grass, until we were looking down over an empty white beach. It was empty of people, but studded with stumps of wood, broken breakwaters.

"Rotting groynes," he said. Well, afterwards, I realised that he'd said that, but at the time I heard it differently. I don't know what expression must have crossed my face. Kissing one minute and then talking about rotting groins? One of those images of the symptoms of venereal disease came into my mind. That was in a book someone had been browsing last week. I couldn't help thinking that if it had been me, I'd have put it back on the shelf myself and not left it out for someone else to put away. It made me think about the sex education lessons we had at school. They seemed to be all about sexually transmitted diseases, as far as I can remember. I suppose it was the same time as the Aids scare. I'll never forget that advert with the big black monolith. 'Don't die of ignorance' was the message, I think. I must have only been about twelve, and ignorant of so many things.

Right now, I was wondering whether I'd somehow put Neil off when he kissed me. He hadn't seemed disgusted, though. I thought of doing that thing teenagers do when they breathe into cupped hands to see if their breath smells. But then you don't run off to brush your teeth just because you think someone might want to kiss you any minute. Though he hadn't seemed disgusted at all. Quite the opposite. So why was he now striding off ahead again?

He remained an enigma to me. Despite the fact that I couldn't help bombarding him with questions, what did I really know about him? And he showed little or no curiosity about me, just accepting my presence as a given. I suspected he never even thought about me when I wasn't there.

It seemed that there was to be no more handholding. No romantic stroll along the beach together. No walking into the sunset. The sun was sinking into a grey mist that seemed to rise up from the water and the low-lying land.

I'd only just caught up with him when we got to the road that led from the village to the beach. It ended suddenly with a jagged edge at the edge of the cliff. Below, the beach was strewn with huge lumps of concrete and broken road. A caravan park was perched perilously close to the cliff edge, but the pitches nearest the edge lay vacant, as deep cracks in the ground snaked towards them.

We stopped at the visitor centre on the corner of the road. On the side of the building there were two plaques. One said that it had been built 534 yards from the sea in 1917. The other that it was 190 yards from the sea when it was restored in 1994. I wondered how close it was to the sea now. Would it fall over the edge one day, like the road and so much else?

Inside the visitor centre there was a model of the peninsula. It showed how this finger of land had shifted naturally over the years, but that attempts to stabilise it meant that it was now in danger of being completely breached by the sea.

"I shall miss coming here," Neil said suddenly, as we sat over a pot of tea, looking out at the rapidly advancing sea, which was now disappearing into mist and the encroaching darkness.

"Why? I mean, won't you be coming back here?"

He pulled an envelope out of his pocket and passed it to me. I opened it and read the letter. It was a job offer for a teaching post on the Isle of Mull, in Scotland.

I felt the cold mist start to seep into the café.

"Are you accepting it?" I asked.

He nodded. "Already have done. I had to hand in my notice at half term. I can't wait. It starts in January. But I'm moving as soon as this school term finishes for Christmas."

"But what about… your house?"

"Oh, I'm just going to rent it to Dan, while I look for somewhere up there."

"So, you intend to stay there?"

"Too right. It's my dream. I can't believe it's finally happened."

So that was his dream. I wanted to ask what about us? But was there even an 'us'?

"Well, that's great," I said, hoping I didn't sound sarcastic. "Shall I see you again before you go?"

"Not sure. It's a pretty busy time at school. But hey, you'll have to come up and visit me. I'll send you my address once I'm sorted."

"Yes, that would be nice."

CHAPTER FOURTEEN

Another Conversation

So that was that. I felt that it had no sooner started than it had ended. Whatever *it* was. Another door closed.

I tried to throw myself into work, but whatever I did, it reminded me of Neil. Everything I read seemed to have some kind of link to Scotland or birds or eroding coastlines or even Tolkien.

On November 20th we found out that Hull was going to be UK City of Culture in 2017. It felt like the whole city was on a high. There would be plans to make, events to organise. We were all going to be part of it.

But I didn't feel part of it at all. My mind was elsewhere.

I was also worried about my nan, who seemed less and less willing to leave the house.

"In the spring," she said, "when it's warmer." She'd always seemed so resilient, but now she seemed to be growing tired.

I thought back to what she'd said about when she'd had her baby, during the war. About how cold it was. Any attempts I'd made to ask her about it again had been rapidly deflected. She was more interested in Neil.

"It's not going to happen, Nan," I confided one day.

"Oh, why ever not? He seemed such a nice young man, and I can tell you liked him. Have you fallen out or something?"

"No, it's not that. He's moving away. To Scotland."

"Well, that's not the end of the world. You could always follow him there. If you really wanted to."

"What and leave you? And my job?"

"Oh, don't you worry about me. It's time you started thinking about your own life. I'm sure they have libraries in Scotland. And it's not like you're getting any younger."

"Says you."

"Oh, I've had my time. I've had a good life really. But you, you haven't even started yours. It's no good thinking of starting a family when you're middle aged. It's all right for the men. They don't hear the clock ticking in the same way. Just don't leave it till too late."

She stopped. I think she'd noticed I was welling up. "Sorry duck, I didn't mean to upset you. What is it?"

How could I explain what I didn't understand myself? I hadn't even known I wanted a child until I'd had that conversation with Neil. And I still didn't know. I didn't know what I wanted. Did I want to be with Neil, regardless? Well. it wasn't even an issue. Neil had made it clear that I wasn't part of his vision of the future. He just saw me as a friend, someone nice to be with, but easily forgotten the moment we weren't together.

"Nan, do you ever think about your first sweetheart, that man you met during the war? Do you think you might have stayed together if he hadn't gone away?"

"I don't know, love. I don't even know what happened to him. But it was different in the war. There were so many partings, and it kind of made everyone feel more alive, as if you had to make the most of your time together. I suppose that's why we got carried away and went too far. I wasn't the only one to be left in the pudding club." She laughed. "That's what we used to call it!"

I was glad she was laughing.

"So, it wasn't all bad, then?

"Oh, we had a laugh sometimes, us girls, But you know we weren't supposed to. It was all scrubbing and cleaning. And walking to church in a crocodile! Can you imagine? So that everyone could see our shame?"

"Where was it, Nan?"

"Why, it was just off Hessle Road. Not far from where we lived, before we moved here. All gone now."

"Wasn't that a bit near home? I thought you said you got sent away. What if people saw you?"

"Well, you know, our house was outside of town, in Hessle. It might have been at the other end of the country for all I saw of my mam and dad. It was as if I was dead to them all the time that I was there. And it was the war, remember. Did I ever tell you about the night they dropped a bomb on Corporation buses? The sky was all red with the fire and the smoke. You could see it from Hessle."

More and more she seemed to want to talk about the past, until I asked her about her baby, and then she would just clam up or pointedly change the subject, like someone closing a door.

CHAPTER FIFTEEN

Deluged

My conversation with Nan may have taken my mind off Neil for the moment, but it hadn't stopped me thinking about the way I'd reacted when he'd said he didn't want children. It was as if it had triggered something in myself. I'd never seen myself as someone who might get broody. I'd see plenty of kids on the estate, riding their bikes on the pavement, older ones gathering on street corners and outside the shops. Then there were the schoolchildren that visited the library for author visits. It was always a relief when they left; I'd never fancied being a teacher. And the whining toddlers that were brought into the library? None of them would have made me broody. Quite the opposite in fact.

I found myself wondering what would have happened if I'd not had the abortion. Forgetting Alan for the moment, what if I'd gone ahead and had a baby, just by myself, without involving Alan in any way? My mum would have stood by me, just like my nan stood by her. But I didn't want to be like my mum. It seemed to me that her life had closed in on her just when it should have been getting started. Again, I found myself wondering about what my nan had gone through, when she gave up her baby. What had happened to him or her?

Back at work, I decided to return to my research. It turned out there was another maternity home in Hull run by the Church. The York Diocesan Maternity Home opened in 1915, and it was still operating in the 1970s, but under a different name. So, it must have been there during the war. I looked up Linnaeus Street, where it was sited, on Google Maps. It was in that area that used to be the hub of the old Hessle Road, all long-since demolished and replaced by blocks of flats and more modern terraces. The street must have seen some changes from when it was the heart of the fishing community. It was only a few streets away from the Boulevard, where Mum had lived when she fell pregnant with me in 1974. I wondered if she knew about it. Most excitingly, there were surviving admission and discharge books from 1940 to 1945. Maybe I could actually find out what happened to Nan's baby. I knew her maiden name was Jackson.

Should I have carried on looking? Nan was obviously happy to let sleeping dogs lie, to leave the past undisturbed. But I couldn't. For some reason, I had to carry on. It was as if that first meeting with Jim, my self-professed dad, had awakened in me this ferocious thirst to find out about my family and all its secrets. Or maybe it was just a way of escaping from my own problems.

My investigations were interrupted by a customer, Marjorie Davies. She always borrows books from the large-print section. Always historical romances. She's a particular fan of Valerie Wood, a local author. Usually, I'm happy to chat to her about the books, but today I couldn't wait for her to leave. She seemed a bit reluctant.

"Do you know, I don't fancy going out into that wind again. I could hardly keep my feet."

"Yes, I noticed it was windy this morning. Well, take care, and go straight home if it's still bad. We don't want you getting blown over."

I was busy with library work for an hour or two, and then I returned to my research. Where could I find these records? To my disappointment, they were not held at the Hull History Centre, which I could easily have accessed, but at the Borthwick Institute for Archives at the University of York. I tried to access the information online, but I ran up against a blank wall. Whatever I entered in the search bar, nothing came up.

I decided to ring Amy. She's an old friend from college. We did our training together and we'd shared a flat for a while. She moved to the History Centre when it opened a few years ago. Before that, she worked in the archives under the City Hall. Sometimes we'd organise visits together for parties of school children. They were usually doing a history project on the war, and she'd get out all the old maps that show where the bombs fell. If anyone could find what I needed, she could.

She wasn't surprised to hear from me, or to discover that I needed her to find something out. But when I told her that I was looking for information about a Doris Jackson, she put two and two together.

"Doris? Is that your grandma? Are you getting into family history, then?" she asked.

"Yes, do you mind? I just need to find out if she was admitted to the maternity home sometime in early 1942. I think her baby was born in January." I remembered Nan saying how cold it was. I pictured a cheerless dormitory, presided over by an equally cold and disapproving matron, and shivered.

"No worries. Leave it with me. Do you fancy meeting up sometime for a drink?"

"Well, actually I might pop into town after work, today. Why don't we meet up in the Old English Gentleman? About half past five?"

"Great idea. I'll see what I can find out this afternoon. By the way, how's your friend?"

"Who?"

"The good-looking teacher guy you sent to see me. You can send me more like him."

"Oh, I don't know. I don't really see him anymore."

"Shame."

"Don't forget you're supposed to be married, Amy."

"Tell that to Richard," she said.

"What? Are things okay with you two?"

"Oh, you know, men. I'll tell you later."

As soon as I'd finished work, I caught the bus into town. Marjorie was right about the wind. I struggled to keep my balance at the bus stop as the wind swept across the flat streets of the estate.

It was a relief to be snugly ensconced in the cluttered interior of the Old English Gentleman. Signed photographs of famous actors looked down from the walls. Being situated just round the corner from the New Theatre, the pub has always attracted the theatrical crowd. I wondered who had stayed in its rooms over the years.

Amy arrived a few minutes later, looking windswept after only walking across the courtyard from the History Centre.

"So, what's up with you and Richard?" I asked, as I took a sip of beer.

"Oh, I don't know really. It's just that he's never home. Always got some meeting or other to go to. I mean I'm used to him working in the evenings. That's what you get when you marry a lecturer. But at least he was working at home. Maybe the job's changed since he got that promotion. I don't know. It's just, we're supposed to be trying for a family, and he gets home so late and then he sits up doing his work, and I'm usually asleep by the time he comes to bed."

I nodded sympathetically. To be fair, I didn't have that much sympathy. I thought she was lucky. She was married to a gorgeous guy. Both of them had good jobs, a nice house. And then I thought about what she'd said.

"You don't think he's seeing someone else, do you?"

"I just don't know. I really don't. I mean, I don't see how he could fit that in along with all his work, but I don't really know what he's doing when he's out all evening, do I? Anyway, enough about me. Do you want to know what I found out?"

"Did you manage to find something?"

"Not just one thing. Two. Twins," she replied, raising her glass in a gesture of celebration.

"Twins? No! Really? She never said."

"Definitely twins. David and John. Born on the twenty-second of January nineteen forty-two."

"I can't believe it. She had twins and she never said. I mean she never said it wasn't, but I just assumed. To be fair, she didn't really say very much. Did you find anything else out? Do you know what happened to them?"

"Let me see. I wrote it down for you, here. Yes, David was adopted – it didn't name the adoptive parents. And John went to Hesslewood Orphanage."

"But he wasn't an orphan! His mother was still alive. And he had a father somewhere."

"I don't think that mattered. If the mother couldn't keep the baby and they couldn't find a family to adopt, the baby would be taken into care. Fostered or sent to an orphanage. What a pity that both babies couldn't have been adopted. It seems really sad that they were separated."

"And Hesslewood Orphanage – do you have any records?"

"Well, oddly enough, we get quite a lot of enquiries, so I know the answer to that. We've got all the admissions registers, birth and baptism certificates. Even the punishment book!"

I shuddered. Poor little John. What would it have been like for him at the orphanage? I wonder if Nan knew that he'd ended up there. Did she ever wonder what happened to them? Or did she just shut off that line of thought? I felt a wave of gratitude that my mum hadn't had to go through anything like that, that my nan had been there for her.

"Of course, we can't share the information with the public. The records are closed under the data protection act. We can share them with relatives, but only if they can provide a death certificate, to show that the person is deceased."

"Oh, I see. What about the one that was adopted? David?"

"It's really tricky. The problem is that the adoptive parents usually changed the child's name. Sometimes not just the surname but the first name as well, especially if it was a baby."

Well, I'd found some answers. Maybe it was nothing that Nan didn't know, but she was obviously keeping it to herself if she did. But I'd come up against another dead end. I wondered if David and John were still alive. How old would they be now? Seventy-one, nearly seventy-two. My family seemed to be growing by the minute. First, I find someone claiming to be my father, and then I discover I have two uncles I didn't know about!

Funny though. There was something about that date, January 22nd, that seemed familiar. What was it?

Amy had left. She was driving so she didn't want to stay out. But I ordered another drink, a pint this time. I wasn't in any hurry to leave, and I didn't fancy standing at another bus-stop in that weather. I thought about Nan. She would be okay, probably dozing in front of the TV as usual, spilling her cup of tea as she nodded off.

There was a clatter, as a sign or something blew over outside.

January 22nd. What was it about that date? I looked up at the faces of the famous stars. None of them seemed to have the answer I was looking for, but I always enjoyed looking at them. It was one of my favourite pubs. That and the Old Town pubs down their secret alleyways: the Olde Black Boy on High Street and the Olde White Hart on Silver Street. It was there in the plotting parlour that plans were made to prevent the king from entering the city during the Civil War.

Secrets, plots and treasonous acts.

When I was with Alan, we always had to visit out-of-the-way pubs where no one would recognise us. There was one down Wincolmlee, the Whalebone. The walls were lined with black and white photos of old Hull pubs and local football and rugby league teams. Then there was the Minerva, down at the pier, with its pictures of old trawlers. I wondered if it had a photo of the Gaul. I couldn't remember whether I'd seen one. It wasn't as if it had even been an old trawler. That was the awful thing about it.

But there was something about the Gaul. And that date. I wished I'd got myself a smart phone. It never seemed necessary, with me having all the access to the internet I needed at work. I just had a normal phone. But more and more people had them. Like that woman at the bar. She was showing something on her phone to her friend and they were laughing. They looked quite approachable. As I went up to order another drink, I asked her outright.

"Excuse me, but I don't suppose I could borrow your phone for a second, could I? I just really need to check something."

"Yeah, okay. Wifi signal isn't great though."

I searched 'Gaul Trawler' and skimmed through the Wikipedia entry looking for dates. There it was, under 'Final Voyage': *Gaul sailed from Hull on the morning of 22 January 1974.* Well, that was a weird coincidence.

"Can I just check something else?" I asked.

"Go on, then." She turned to her companion, and they carried on their conversation. She must have trusted me not to steal her phone.

What had Jim said about the day it sailed? That it was his birthday? I tried to remember where I'd found the crew list, but although there was plenty about the Gaul, I couldn't find the list of names I'd seen before. Still, it didn't matter. It was just a coincidence. A coincidence that my father and my uncles had the same birthday.

James Thompson. David Jackson. John Jackson.

People called John were sometimes called Jack. Jim had talked about Jack being his doppelganger. Could Jack have been his twin? John Jackson?

My head was spinning. What had Meg said about adopted babies? About their surnames and first names sometimes being changed? And what had Jim said about being adopted? And about Jack being brought up in care?

Surely, it was more than coincidence. But if it was…

"Excuse me, but have you finished with my phone?"

I realised I was still holding it,

"Oh, sorry. Yes…"

"Did you find what you were looking for?"

"No. I mean, yes. No, it doesn't matter."

She looked at me rather oddly as I returned her phone, and then turned back to her companion.

* * *

I don't know how much I drank, but when I left the pub, I could hardly walk. Or maybe that was just the wind. It was cold and salty on my face, as if it had blown straight off the sea. I saw the headlights of a taxi approaching and held my hand out to stop it.

"Where to, love?"

"Hessle Road. Rayners."

I don't know why I said that. I knew I should have gone home, but I couldn't. Not yet. I wasn't ready to see Nan or talk to her about what I'd found out.

As I was getting out, the taxi-driver was telling me something, something about the storm and a tidal surge, but I wasn't listening. My thoughts were lurching, like a ship thrown about by the waves. I needed to feel the wind in all its fury, as it propelled me down the street. What direction was it taking me in? Where was I heading? I wanted not to know what I now knew or suspected. I wanted answers, but at the same time I didn't want them. What answers was I looking for now, here on Hessle Road? It wasn't the community that my mum grew up in anymore. It was just like any other street. No sharp-suited three-day millionaires drinking away their money. It didn't even smell of fish anymore.

But it still smelt of the sea, and today more than ever. Maybe it was the wind.

I suddenly realised my feet were wet. I looked around. It was dark, much darker than it should have been, and I saw that the streetlights were off, and some of the buildings were in darkness. There were lights from cars, but confused, as if they were turning and heading off in panic. Or was that sense of panic coming from the siren, that high wailing sound I could hear?

Had I somehow gone back in time to the Blitz? The blackout, the sirens…what did they mean? Where was this water coming from? It was nearly up to my knees now. I didn't know which way to turn. Ahead of me, a car sputtered to a halt, the water up to its wheel arches. Beyond it, a chaos of abandoned cars, people shouting.

And my thoughts were still spinning and clashing around in my head. Could Jim have slept with his own half-sister? What did that mean? For him? For me? What could I tell Nan? That she has a son that's alive and well but living a false life, and one that's dead, that was a liar and a thief?

And what about Jim? Should I tell him he's not only got a daughter but a birth mother that's still alive?

As the icy water swirled around my legs, I realised I was shaking with cold. I felt myself sinking, being swept along. There was no time to think. I had to get out of this first.

CHAPTER SIXTEEN

It Ends

I remember waking up in bed. When I tried to sit up, my head was still spinning. Was I still drunk? How had I got home? My throat felt raw, and I reached out gratefully for the glass of water next to my bed.

I was aching in every joint. What had happened?

The next few days were a bit of a blur. I remember my nan bringing me drinks as I drifted in and out of sleep. It turned out I was actually ill, not just suffering a massive hangover.

Then one day, I woke up and realised my mind had cleared. I sat up. I still felt weak, but definitely more myself again.

My nan came into my room.

"How are you feeling, love? Good to see you sitting up. Let me brush your hair for you."

"No, Nan. It's not right. I should be looking after you."

"Now you know you don't need to worry about me. I can get by. Do you think you might come downstairs for a bit? Have a change of scene?"

I carried my duvet downstairs with me and wrapped it round me on the sofa. I was still feeling seriously disorientated and a bit wobbly.

"What day is it, Nan? How long have I been ill?"

"Now, let me see. Where are my glasses?" She always says that, even though they're round her neck on a string. She picked up the newspaper, which was turned to the TV page. "Ah yes, it's Monday. Monday the ninth of December."

"But that means it's been three days, no, four! Nan, what about work?"

"Now don't you worry about that. They rang up and I told them you were poorly. A touch of flu, I said. Now just you concentrate on getting better."

"Nan, I'm sorry. You shouldn't have had to look after me."

"And who else was going to look after you? I'm just glad to see you up and about again. Gave me a bit of a fright, I can tell you, seeing you drenched to the bone like that."

I tried to think back. I'd had so many confusing dreams over the last few days, I wasn't sure what had been dream and what had been reality. I remembered being swept along in the water and darkness. There was a lot of shouting or screaming. Was that me? Then there was someone else there. Maybe two people. I remembered being dragged by the arms, my legs not working, and being bundled into a car.

"Nan? Who brought me home?"

"Why, it was those nice police officers. A lady and a young fella. I offered them a cup of tea, once we got you sorted. Looked like they could do with one, but they said no. They had to get back. Rather them than me, I thought. It was wild out there. Anyways I was glad they got you home. What a state you were in. You looked like death warmed up. They said you'd got caught up in them floods on Hessle Road. But I could see you weren't right at all. They helped me get your wet clothes off you and get you up to your bed. Well, I couldn't have done it by myself, and you were in no fit state. Now, what on earth sent you wandering round Hessle Road in that weather?"

As she told me about it, I knew it was true. There were little bits of memory that came floating back to me. I remembered leaving the Old English Gentleman and getting a taxi. But why hadn't I gone home then? What was I doing on Hessle Road? And why was it so dark? And where had all that water come from? I remembered feeling completely overwhelmed. There was something else as well, but I couldn't think what it was.

I looked at the pile of newspapers stacked up on the side table. We got the local paper delivered every day because Nan liked to have the TV page and to look at the flashback features on Hull in the old days, and I tried to keep up with local events. People expected librarians to be the fount of all knowledge.

I flicked through them. The tidal surge on December 5th had been caused by Storm Xavier hitting the East Coast. Although the tidal barrier had been lowered, to stop the River Hull flooding the old town, it hadn't stopped the River Humber overtopping Albert Dock, the old fishing dock behind Hessle Road. I realised I'd been up to my knees in the North Sea.

The storm and tidal surge had been front page news, pushing into insignificance the fact that Nelson Mandela had died on the same day. Spurn point had been breached, becoming an island, just as Neil had predicted.

It took a couple more days for me to feel like myself. I dragged myself into work, and then just slumped on the sofa when I got home. I should have paid more attention to my nan, but I suppose I'd got used to taking her for granted over the years. She kept insisting I needed to rest, and I was just relieved that she didn't seem to have caught the flu or whatever I'd had. She would fall asleep every evening in front of the TV, and I suspected she slept through the afternoons as well. I did feel guilty that she'd had to look after me while I was ill, but there was nothing I could do about it. At least I knew I'd been properly ill and not just suffering the hangover from Hell.

It was on the Thursday, I think, that I was half-heartedly watching Look North when I realised, with a jolt, that they were talking about the Gaul. Ten bodies had been found in a Russian cave. Tests were being conducted to see if they were the missing crew members.

It all came back to me in a rush. What I'd found out. The man who had taken my dad's place on the Gaul was his twin brother, my uncle...

My nan was just coming into the room with a cup of tea for both of us. I noticed how frail and tired she looked. It was as if I was seeing her with fresh eyes. Had I forgotten how old she was? Or had she exhausted herself, looking after me? I felt a rush of guilt.

"Sit down, Nan. You shouldn't be waiting on me."

It was her who broached the subject of the Gaul: "I don't know why they want to dredge all this up. We need to let it go. I know it's sad, but they're gone and that's all there is to it. The past is the past."

"Nan, there's something I need to tell you."

"Well, before you do that, I've just remembered there's a letter for you. Now where did I put it?"

I recognised the handwriting immediately. Making an excuse, I picked up my cup of tea and the letter and headed up to my room.

"Is it a love letter, pet?" I heard Nan call after me. "Is it from that nice young man?"

It was shorter than Jim's previous letter.

My dear Helen

I cannot tell you how happy I am to have met you, but it's enough for me to have done so. I realise now that you have your own life, and I don't want to force myself into it after all this time. I have also made my own life, across the river, and I'm happy in it. Don't feel that you have to look out for me. I have my friends. And you will have yours. The past is the past.

Your loving dad

Jim

How did I feel when I read those words? Rejected? Relieved? How strange that he had echoed Nan's words about the past. Like mother, like son?

I stayed there a long time. But as I sat on my bed, looking at his words, I felt a gradual clearing of my mind. It was as if the swirling flood waters subsided. It didn't matter. None of it mattered. I had my nan, and my memories of my mum. I'd met my dad, and he was a good man. He was no longer a shadow from the past. Nor did my discovery need to cast a shadow on the future.

When I went back downstairs, much later, I saw that Nan had nodded off again, spilling her cup of tea. It must have gone quite cold. Her mouth had fallen open as it so often did when she fell asleep. I took the cup and saucer from her hands. And realised that they too were cold.

She'd been telling me for a long time that she was tired. I knew that old age had finally caught up with her, but somehow I'd thought she'd go on for ever. How like her to have used her last ounce of energy looking after me.

I'd got used to her sleeping more and more, but this time, I realised, she wouldn't be waking up.

CHAPTER SEVENTEEN

In Limbo

I knew immediately that she'd gone, and I knew with equal certainty that it was the right time for her. It was as if she'd just waited until I was on my feet again and then let go. The TV had turned itself off while I had been upstairs, and for a moment, there was complete silence.

Then it was as if my brain started up again. What was the right thing to do? Should I ring 999? 111? Her doctor? She looked so peaceful, but should I have tried to revive her? The calmness that had pervaded the room was replaced by a sense of panic. Why did I have to do this by myself?

I rang the doctor and tried to explain. No, she wasn't breathing. For how long? I didn't know. I had no idea what time I'd spoken to her. Look North had been on TV. Teatime. She was cold, quite cold. I just wanted someone to come and take over, tell me what to do.

It had been so different when my mum had died. There'd been people around: nurses, people that knew what they were doing. It had been coming for so long, and when it came, it was a kind of relief. She had lost so much weight, was so changed from the person she'd once been. There was all the medical paraphernalia and clutter, and people who took over and gave me advice.

But this time, there was just me, and my nan sitting in her chair, looking just as she always did. I hadn't known that death could creep up on you like that and just tap you on the shoulder, as if to say, 'It's time now'.

And then the world started turning again, and for a while I was too busy to think about it. There were funeral directors to contact and decisions to be made.

I'd gone through the same thing just five years ago when my mum died, but then my nan had been there to support me, to talk it over with, in the same way that she'd always been there for me. We'd discussed what Mum would have wanted, and we'd hugged each other and cried together and laughed sometimes. Then there were mum's friends and neighbours and her colleagues from work, and we'd been like a team putting together the plans for the funeral, making sure it reflected the person we had all known.

But after the undertakers took my nan away, I was alone in the house. And again, for a while, I just froze. The funeral couldn't take place till after Christmas, so I had about three weeks of being in limbo. At least I knew what she wanted. She'd told me often enough, even though I hadn't wanted to listen. Just a simple ceremony at the crematorium.

That was when I had to decide. When the funeral director from the Co-op asked if there were any other family members. I said no automatically. And then I remembered.

"Oh, I mean yes, there is someone. He's…"

What was he? My dad? My uncle? I felt myself drowning once again, a feeling of rising panic engulfing me like flood waters. I should tell Jim. But what should I tell him? That my nan had died, Linda's mum. That he might like to be there. But what was she to him? He'd never met her. No, that wasn't it. She was his mother too. But he didn't know that. I told myself that it wasn't even as if I had any proof that it was true. Though I knew that it was. Did he need to know now? Would she have wanted him to know? There'd always just been the three of us. Me, my mum, my nan. What was he to do with us? I desperately wanted to ask someone for advice, and at the same time I didn't. I needed to work it out for myself.

"Are you all right? Would you like a cup of tea?" I realised that the young woman was looking at me in concern.

"No, no, I'm fine. Sorry, there's something I have to do."

I'd thought when I read that last letter and when my nan died that it was the end of that particular nightmare. I'd thought it was over. I didn't need to worry any more about whether to tell my nan what I'd discovered. When I found out that Jim, my dad, didn't want me to contact him, I'd thought that the rising tide of panic that had swept through me that night had receded for good. But it was still there. And I'd never felt so alone.

I bought myself a bottle of wine and drank it, as I scraped together a meal of what was left in the fridge. I put both of Jim's letters in front of me and read them again. His number was still there. I could ring. I could text him and ask him to meet me. I could just send a text. But to say what?

Thanks for your letter. I just thought I should let you know that my nan died last week. Funeral at Hull Crematorium January 4ᵗʰ 2pm.

There, I'd told him. Only I hadn't told him anything really. But at least I'd told him. Maybe if he came to the funeral, I would tell him then. Depending on how it went. If it seemed right. Yes, that's what I would do. It was a relief not to have to do anything immediately.

CHAPTER EIGHTEEN

A Family Gathering

I was dreading my first Christmas by myself. It wasn't as if I was part of a large family. Huge gatherings had never been my experience of Christmas, but we'd celebrated it our own way, just the three of us, and then me and my nan. In recent years, she hadn't got out to the shops anymore, but she'd tell me to buy myself something nice and then she'd wrap it up for me. She'd enjoy a glass of sherry, and we'd have a proper Christmas dinner followed by the Queen's speech. Then we'd watch a film on TV, and she would fall asleep with her teacup on her lap. Nan used to insist that she wanted to help me with the dinner and clearing up afterwards, but she didn't really have the energy anymore. It was enough for her to lay the table. She always took a pleasure in setting out her best china that only came out on special occasions.

Sometimes I used to wonder what had become of my life, that I was celebrating Christmas with just an old lady for company. I don't know what I'd imagined my life would be like by the time I was in my late thirties, but I suppose I'd always thought that I'd end up married, in my own home and, yes, with children. Not loads of children, I couldn't imagine that. But especially after Mum died, I kind of thought that I'd take over that role myself one day.

Then two days before Christmas, I got a call from Amy. It turned out that her husband, Richard, had just up and left, only days after I'd met up with her at the Old English Gentleman. Apparently, he'd gone off with an ex-student, fifteen years his junior. What made it worse was that he'd been seeing her for some time.

"You knew something was wrong when we met up, didn't you? I suppose you just didn't want to believe that he'd do such a thing."

"I can't believe I didn't realise," she told me. "I must have been blind. And now I can't believe he's gone. I mean, the house feels so empty."

"I know what you mean." I told her about losing my nan.

"Oh, Helen, I'm so sorry. There's me going on about myself, and look what's happened to you! I know, why don't you come to mine on Christmas Day? I'm afraid there'll be a bit of a crowd. My mum insisted on coming over with my dad and my brother. Oh, and their dog will be coming too. A bit smelly, but he's okay. The dog, I mean, not my brother, though maybe him as well. Anyway, it'll be better than being by yourself. And to be honest, it'd be better for me. My mum can be a bit full on, if you know what I mean."

I didn't, but I accepted the invitation anyway. I couldn't think how else I'd spend the day. I'd known of course that my nan wouldn't be around for ever, but I'd probably imagined that when that time came, I'd be in a relationship of my own. I'd even dreamt of spending

Christmas in some exotic place abroad or watching the Northern Lights on a romantic winter holiday. I certainly hadn't pictured myself watching TV alone at home.

It was hard to believe that Richard had left Amy. They'd been together for years and always seemed perfectly matched: him a History lecturer, her working at the History Centre. They'd bought a house together and had been doing it up. It was the sort of house I'd have loved to live in, full of books and plants. I knew they'd been trying for a family. But now this. I guess you never really know what's going on in someone else's relationship, behind closed doors.

Then of course the whole thing made me think back to Alan, when I'd been the Other Woman, I suppose. But I didn't see myself as a marriage wrecker. And anyway, I hadn't wrecked anyone's marriage. If there'd been a casualty in that relationship it had been me. And the baby I never had.

Maybe Richard wouldn't have left Amy if they'd really been meant for each other. You can't always judge from the outside. But how could you know if you'd found the right person? There again, maybe Richard was just a bastard. I wondered what my nan would have said.

"Men!" she'd have sniffed. "We're better off without them." Well, she hadn't exactly had a good experience of men in her life, though she never gave up hoping I'd find Mr Right. She'd taken quite a shine to Neil, but where was he now?

Yes, it would definitely be a good distraction to spend Christmas at Amy's, however ghastly her family might turn out to be.

* * *

"We couldn't leave you to rattle round in this house by yourself, could we?" Amy's mother said to her, pouring herself a large glass of sherry. I could see Amy thinking it wouldn't have been such a bad thing after all. Her mother mostly swanned around, glass in hand, expressing surprise at the contents of Amy's kitchen and at her cooking methods, but providing very little practical help. She kept up a continual stream of conversation, more of a monologue really, but I suppose she meant well. She'd heard I'd just lost my nan.

"And Amy tells me you've got no other family. Well, that's a real shame for you. And you haven't got a fella either? Look at both of you, no children, no fella, and nearly forty. Of course, Amy did have a fella, but he wasn't much use, was he? All very well for him. He's got all the time in the world, men do. But not us women. I said to Amy she needs to get a move on and find someone sharpish or it'll be too late. I'd been married to your father for fifteen years when I was your age. And I'm not complaining, but I'm in my sixties now and where are my grandchildren?"

"Mum, that's not helpful, you know."

"Well, someone has to say it. Of course, it's different for men. Now look at Max, for instance. He's just getting ready to settle down. Plenty of time to sow his wild oats. Not that I've seen him sowing any. Spends too much time on his computer. About time he moved out, I tell him, found himself a nice girl and settled down. He's never going to meet anyone if he never goes anywhere, is he?"

I nodded vaguely in agreement. Max was sprawled on the bit of the sofa that wasn't occupied by the dog, glued to his phone. From what I'd heard of him, he probably wasn't texting his friends. More likely he was playing some geeky game. From the moment I'd shaken his rather clammy hand, I'd decided to give him a wide berth.

That wasn't so easy however when we were all sat round the table. I'd been placed next to him, and he kept filling up my glass, despite my attempts to cover it with my hand. For his part he was glugging away and becoming increasingly voluble, mainly reeling off a series of facts and statistics that no one was interested in.

Meanwhile Amy's mum continued her monologue.

Meg's dad, Colin, just tucked into his dinner, with the occasional murmur of appreciation. I wondered what was actually going on in his head. Occasionally his wife would ask him to corroborate something she'd just said.

"Did you know," said Max, "that ten million turkeys are killed every year at Christmas?"

"Well, I always say," said his mother, "you can judge a Christmas dinner by the quality of the gravy. Isn't that right, Colin?"

"Yes dear. Very nice gravy, Amy."

I doubt he was even listening. Familiarity breeding contempt. Or maybe just creating a kind of ease. Maybe he found it quite restful not having to contribute anything to the conversation. I guess he'd got used to his wife's stream of consciousness, and she was clearly oblivious to whether or not anyone was actually listening. In fact, she and Max were quite similar, the way they talked at you, rather than to you.

She continued, "Now the way I see it, there's nothing wrong with using a couple of spoons of granules. That way you don't get lumps. I mean it's all very well following your Delia Smiths and your Jamie Olivers and suchlike, but sometimes you just need to keep it simple.

Remember that, Amy, next time. Men like a nice bit of gravy."

"Did you know," said Max, "that more than 400,000 illnesses are caused by spoilt Christmas leftovers?"

Well, I suppose it was his way of being festive. Maybe he'd been swotting up on fun facts about Christmas on his phone. It wasn't long before he was reading out the trivia from the Christmas crackers, the ones that you expect to be a joke and wonder why they're not funny. (Then you find the ones that are supposed to be jokes and they're still not funny).

At some point, Amy and I caught each other's eye and started to giggle helplessly. Encouraged by this, Max started telling jokes, while his mother said. "I don't know what you two girls find so funny. I'm only trying to give you a few pointers."

At which point Amy gave a sort of snort and exploded into helpless laughter, which then set me off.

"Here's another one," said Max. "What do you call an old snowman?"

"This wine's a bit tart," said his mother.

"Water," said Max, and then when nobody laughed, he explained, "because it's melted."

After dinner, Amy's dad settled into the armchair and was soon snoring contentedly. Max was following me round, trying to persuade me to drink something noxious from a dark blue bottle, so I escaped into the kitchen to help with the washing up. Amy's mum continued to proffer advice. "I'm always telling Amy she should wear rubber gloves when she's washing up. Just look how dry her hands are getting. Hand cream and rubber gloves, that's the secret."

I knew Amy would have liked to talk to me alone, but it was hopeless. Still, it took my mind off the funeral. And Jim. And everything I'd discovered just three weeks earlier.

CHAPTER NINETEEN

Saying Goodbye

The funeral itself was very quiet. Nan had reached that age when the people she used to know had moved away or died. But at least I got to say goodbye.

The neighbours turned up. Amy came, which was nice. But there was no other family. I kept looking out for Jim, but he didn't come. It was a relief really, but I couldn't help feeling somewhere a sense of disappointment.

Afterwards I just went for a drink with Amy.

"I'm sorry about Christmas," she said.

"Oh, it's okay. It was quite funny really. Took my mind off things. What about you?"

"To be honest, I'm still struggling with it. I mean, all those years we spent together. What was it all for? I can't help wondering if it'd been different if we'd tried for a family earlier on. Maybe he wouldn't have left if we'd had kids. But I never even really thought about it when I was in my twenties. Neither of us did. And then we said we'd get a house first and get it done up. And then we were waiting for Richard to get a senior lectureship so that we could manage on one income if we needed to. And then we started trying for a family and it didn't happen."

"Do you think that's why he left?"

"I don't know. I just keep asking myself if he was disappointed in me somehow. I don't even know what he really wanted. Did I just assume he wanted kids? Is that why he left? Because we weren't on the same page? Or did he really, really want kids and thought I'd let him down?"

"I think you're overthinking it," I said. "Maybe he just fancied this girl and mistook it for a grand passion. Maybe when the novelty's worn off, he'll realise what he's lost. Typical man." I realised I was sounding like my nan. Or was it my mum? "Anyway, you shouldn't ask me for advice. I'm not exactly the world's expert on successful relationships, am I?"

"That reminds me. You never told me what happened with handsome teacher guy."

"Oh, he was just another one that got away. I thought we actually had something, and then he suddenly announced he was clearing off to Scotland, as if that had nothing to do with me at all."

"Men. Who needs them, eh? Talking of which, what did you think of my lovely brother?"

"Erm, possibly not quite my type? I hope you weren't trying to do a spot of matchmaking there."

"Don't worry. He's a hopeless case. I think he'll be living at home when he's fifty. Mind, I think my mum might have tried to play cupid if I'd let her. Sorry about her, by the way."

"Actually, I quite liked her really. I was thinking about it afterwards. You know, she really cares about you, Amy. I think she just wants you to be happy."

"And to give her some grandchildren."

"Well, yes, that as well. And your dad. He doesn't say much, but I could see he was trying to show you how much he appreciated the dinner, despite what your mum said about it."

"I know, they're an odd couple really, but I suppose they rub along all right. You know, I thought Richard and I would be like that. Well, not like them, obviously. God forbid that I turn into my mum. But I kind of imagined us growing old together. And now what? Do I have to start dating again? I don't even know how to go about it."

"We'll have to go out together. On the pull."

"Like we used to. Remember when we were the Spice Girls? Or the Twice Spice. I was Posh and you were Baby."

"Oh God, don't remind me. I tell you what I want, what I really, really want."

"So tell me what you want, what you really, really want."

Maybe it was odd that we ended up having a laugh together, the day we'd said goodbye to my nan, but I think it cheered us both up. Afterwards I found myself thinking again about Amy and her family. I know her brother was a bit weird, but what was it like to have a sibling? I'd always taken it for granted that I was an only child, just like my mum was. Or thought she was, at any rate.

I thought about the connection that Jim and his brother Jack felt when they met, even though they'd not grown up together. But they weren't similar at all, except in appearance. Even on my short acquaintance with him, I could tell Jim would never have done what Jack did.

And then it turned out that my mum was his half-sister and she never guessed. But then why would she?

I thought about Amy and Max. It was hard to see what they had in common, apart from their parents.

I couldn't imagine what it would have been like to have a father living in the house with us. I suppose we'd have lived somewhere else. My mum only moved back in with my nan because she was a single parent. And my grandad had died when I was still a baby. I remembered what my nan had said about him falling down the stairs when he was drunk.

In some ways I think I was closer to my nan than I was to my mum. It was her that looked after me when Mum was at work or when she went out in the evenings. Funny, I never really thought much about where she went or who she went out with. She never brought anyone back home. There weren't any dodgy so-called uncles hanging around, but she obviously had quite a social life. My nan would as often as not be the one that bathed me and put me to bed. She was the one who had time to sit and listen to me. We'd have tea parties together with my dolls, and she would knit outfits for them.

On the other hand, it was my mum that encouraged me to work hard at school and get qualifications. I liked the way she was strong and independent and didn't have to rely on some man to look after her. And I used to like seeing her dressed smartly for work or all dolled up, as she would say, for a night out.

I remembered my mum's fortieth birthday, even though I must have been quite young. Somehow it stuck in my mind. Her colleagues at the bank gave her a huge card with all their names on it, and on the front, it said 'Life begins at Forty' in big writing. Funny that I should remember that so well. It's just as well she enjoyed life, since it ended so early for her.

And now, my fortieth birthday was approaching, and I had the sense of time ticking by relentlessly. I couldn't even describe myself as young anymore. It was as if another door was closing. A new year and an empty house.

CHAPTER TWENTY

A Journey

In January of 2014, there were more floods in the news. Only this time they were down south, in Somerset. It seemed as if they were on TV every day; even the prime minister was seen wading through the floodwaters in his green wellies. I didn't remember all this attention when Hull flooded back in 2007, even though people were out of their houses for months, some for over a year.

And then in February, the railway line along the Devon coast was washed away. It made me think about my trip to Spurn with Neil, and how the peninsula had now become an island. Maybe he was right to be pessimistic about the future of the planet. Maybe the whole human race would be washed away in another flood like the one in the bible. I imagined Neil as a sort of Noah, with his ark full of endangered species. Though maybe he wouldn't mind a world in which it was just him and the natural world, washed clean of people.

A month or so after my nan died, I texted Neil, just to let him know about what had happened. I thought I should, with him having met her that time. And I said something commonplace, like I hoped he'd settled into his new job and found somewhere to live. I think I was wondering if there was still a connection between us, or if he'd put me out of his mind completely. To my surprise, he replied straightaway,

Sorry to hear about your nan. You'll miss her a lot. You'd like it here. I saw my first sea eagle last week. Neil x

He said I'd like it there. Was that an invite? He had mentioned something before he left about me visiting, but maybe that was just a way of softening the blow when he told me that he was going away. I thought about him quite often. I suppose I had a lot of time to think. Sometimes I considered getting a bus out to the coast so that I could walk along the beach beside the sea that was grey-blue like his eyes. But I didn't, because that would be to admit that I had feelings for him, and he had shown me clearly enough that he was happy to move on, to move away.

Still, I found myself reading about the Isle of Mull, looking at maps and guidebooks. I had this growing feeling that I needed to get away, to see somewhere new. Maybe I would go to Scotland anyway. It didn't need to be Mull. There were plenty of places I could go. I'd never been any further north than Newcastle, and that was for a hen night.

I could visit Edinburgh and then take a train further north to somewhere else. Where did people go? I studied train timetables and started looking for places I could stay. And then gave up. I just had a picture in my mind of me sitting in a soulless hotel room or alone in a bar. I couldn't imagine anything lonelier. So, I forgot about it and concentrated on work and other things. In the evenings I read and watched films, and so the winter passed.

Then I had another text from Neil:

If you fancy a change of scene, I've got time off at Easter.
I could show you the island. You can get a ferry from
Oban x

Now that was definitely an invite. No romantic overtones, apart from the kiss, though that doesn't really count as romantic. I felt it was what I'd been waiting for. I could travel to Oban by train, with three changes. It would take all day, and I'd have to set off early in the morning, but I could be there for the 5 o' clock ferry. Neil said he'd meet me off the ferry on Mull.

As I booked my tickets, I started to feel alive for the first time in ages. It didn't matter how things turned out with Neil; it was just about getting away. I felt like someone in a book, having an actual adventure.

* * *

It was a cold April morning as I got into the taxi that would take me to the station. Fortunately, I'd packed plenty of warm clothes, most of which I'd bought specially for the trip. I'd even bought myself a gigantic rucksack to carry them in. I didn't want Neil thinking I didn't know how to dress for the great outdoors.

The station platform was freezing, but luckily my train was already in, with Hull being a terminus, and it wasn't long before the light flashed up to say that the doors were open.

Once I was ensconced in my seat, with my rucksack stashed away, a coffee in front of me, the feeling of being in a story returned. I found myself mentally describing myself in the third person, like I was a character in a book, and then I ticked myself off and settled down to read. I was reading a novel by Peter May, set on the isle of Lewis. I'd downloaded a whole trilogy on my Kindle. Okay, so Mull was in the Inner Hebrides while Lewis was in the Outer Hebrides, I'd discovered, but it was close enough, I thought, to give me a feel for where I was heading. It was also a crime thriller, so I thought it would keep me engrossed and stop me dwelling on any romantic nonsense. I needed to make sure I didn't fall asleep and forget to change trains at York. There would be further changes at Edinburgh and Glasgow.

Once we'd reached Scotland, I put my Kindle down and just looked out of the window. It had turned into a bright spring day, and I gazed out at the landscape until we entered the urban sprawl of Glasgow.

Somewhere between Glasgow and Oban, the train track ran along the edge of a loch with an impossibly romantic looking castle at its edge. I started to imagine myself as a character in a historical romance. I was with Neil on a craggy hill above the loch, my long flowing gown billowing around me, his fair hair blowing in the wind, as he declared his undying love.

Like that was really going to happen. Still, it was fun to dream. And he had invited me.

It was mid-afternoon when I reached Oban, stepping out of the station to find myself right next to the ferry terminal. Glad of my woolly hat and gloves, not to mention my thick jacket, I bought a coffee and sat at an outside table by the pier, listening to the gulls and taking in the scene: fishing boats in the harbour, mountains in the distance, and what looked like the Coliseum on the hill behind the town.

Once I'd boarded the ferry I went right to the rear deck and watched the waves glittering in the late afternoon sun. We passed a lighthouse on a tiny island of its own. Birds wheeled overhead. Neil would know what they were, I thought. It was really windy, but I didn't care. I'm alive, really alive, I just kept thinking to myself.

Then suddenly there was rain in the wind, and a mass of grey cloud that blotted out the sun. Everyone else seemed to have seen it coming so I was the last person to leave the deck and retreat to the bar.

When we disembarked, I saw him straightaway through the rain, and my stomach did a sort of lurch. He looked exactly the same, except that his hair and beard looked a little wilder than I remembered. He was probably wearing the same clothes as the last time I saw him. Well, it was only a few months ago, but it felt like an age. So much had happened since. He hugged me, gave me a friendly kiss on the cheek and then showed me to a small rather rusty-looking blue car.

"You've got wheels!"

"Well, yes, after a fashion. Actually, it's my neighbour's but they give me the use of it."

Nice neighbours, I thought.

I don't know what I expected of Mull, but this busy stretch of road didn't meet my romantic expectations. Maybe I'd over-imagined the magical experience that this trip would turn out to be. Still, I had come away, and if things didn't work out, I'd lost nothing.

I remembered that Neil had never been a natural behind the wheel. Occasionally he would point out a place where he had seen some bird or other, but I could see nothing through the rain spattered windscreen, and

I had to resist the temptation to tell him to keep his eyes on the road.

Then we turned off onto a narrow single-track road that wound along the side of a river and through a seemingly endless forest. Did Neil actually know where we were going?

Eventually we pulled off the road and into a drive. I could just make out a rather impressive-looking detached house, painted white with pointed eaves above the upstairs windows. "Is this where you live?" I asked.

"Yes," he replied, continuing up the drive to where a caravan was parked. "This is my home."

He explained that his neighbours in the main house rented the caravan out to him. The cost of renting anything else on Mull was out of reach, with so many properties being holiday rentals, and buying was equally impossible.

Inside, the caravan looked more inviting than it did from its exterior, but it was decidedly chilly.

"I'll soon get it warmed up," he said.

Well, there wasn't a lot of it to warm up. Just a couple of seats and a table which I imagined would somehow turn into a bed or beds, a sink, hob, fridge, and what I discovered to be a small but adequate shower cubicle and toilet. There was a tall narrow cupboard, which I presumed was some sort of wardrobe. Good job I didn't bring too much stuff, I thought. Above the seats were shelves, crammed with books and papers, and cupboards that I imagine housed his food supplies.

"Cosy," I said, wondering what sort of guest I was expected to be. Did he think I would be sharing his bed? It was impossible to imagine how we could share this small space without some degree of intimacy. Yet this didn't feel like a romantic tryst. Oh well, I would just see how things turned out. I'd gone back on the pill, just in case. No need for him to know, if nothing happened between us. I wouldn't want him thinking that I'd read more into our relationship than actually existed. Friends, I thought. Rather close friends, as I squeezed next to him in the small space left by my rucksack and his stuff. He'd hung my jacket up in the shower cubicle to dry.

"How do you manage to fit all your stuff in here?" I asked.

"I don't have that much. You know me. I always wear the same things, when I'm not at work. It's surprising how little you need really. I think we've all got too much stuff anyway."

I thought about Nan's stuff that I'd been sorting through at home. She didn't really have all that many possessions either. So much was lost in the floods. And I suppose I didn't have that much to show for my thirty-nine years either. A lot of books, but not much else. I'd never done any of the grown-up things like buying furniture and soft furnishings. My flat had been already furnished and the few bits and pieces I'd bought for it were soon integrated into the house on Northfield when I moved back in with my mum and my nan after the floods. Was it sad to have acquired so little? Neil seemed to find it liberating. And it was an ethical thing for him, not over-consuming, not leaving too heavy a footprint on the planet.

He cooked a sort of camping meal for us, mainly out of tins but hot and extremely welcome after the long day travelling. Clearly this wasn't going to be a gastronomic adventure. Maybe we could eat out in pubs. Did they even have takeaways on this island? Funny, I'd never really thought about Neil in relation to food. I guess it just wasn't one of those things that particularly interested him.

Not that he was without interests. He soon had maps out, spreading them over the little bit of space that we had, pointing out different places that were great for spotting this or that bird. I found myself nodding sleepily. It had been a long day and the van had warmed up nicely. When I let my head rest against Neil's shoulder, he put his arm around me, and I guess we stayed like that for a while.

I must have nodded off, because I woke to find him gently easing me away from him.

"Better set up the bed," he said. "Do you mind sharing?" Having seen the layout of the van, it didn't seem like we had much option. "There is a sort of bunk bed thing that you can pull down, but I doubt if it's very comfortable. I've never used it."

While he was pulling and pushing various things to make the bed, I squeezed into the tiny shower room to undress. I removed my sweater and jeans and decided to keep my tee shirt and underwear on. When I came out, a surprisingly large and comfortable-looking bed was waiting. I climbed in gratefully and nestled down. After a while I was aware that Neil had got in next to me. I still didn't know what he expected, if anything. He was so difficult to read. I pretended to be asleep, until I could hear from his breathing that he had drifted off.

When I woke, he was still lying there next to me. I lay there looking at him for a while, until he opened his eyes. Those eyes that were grey-blue like the North Sea, his fair hair rumpled from sleep. Without thinking, I kissed him lightly on the cheek. "Good morning," I said.

He turned towards me and kissed me, and yes, we made love, in a sort of lazy, sleepy way. I won't say there was passion, because there wasn't. I kept thinking of that phrase I'd always hated, 'friends with benefits'. That's what this felt like. Just two people who liked each other, keeping each other warm. Nothing more. It felt like the most the natural thing in the world, and at the same time it felt like it was nothing important.

CHAPTER TWENTY-ONE

An Island

A nd that was how the week continued. Sometimes I imagined myself having a conversation with my mum.

"Do you like him?" she would ask.

"'Yes, of course," I'd reply.

"And do you fancy him?"

"Definitely yes."

"And is he a good person?"

"Absolutely, yes."

"Well then, what's the problem?"

How could I explain? It was like I knew he wasn't the love of my life, or I of his. We were passing ships. And that was the only reason we could be together like this. I knew he would never ask me to be anything more. And if I suggested to him that we should become... what? An item? Boyfriend and girlfriend? Partners? It was unthinkable. I could imagine how he'd be puzzled, disappointed even.

This was his life: this island, this caravan, his few possessions. And it was somehow too insubstantial for me.

Yes, he wanted to leave a light footprint on the earth, but that meant he didn't seem to want to amount to anything more. It's hard to explain. He didn't want children, he didn't want possessions, he didn't seem bothered about living in a proper house. As for me, I didn't really know what I wanted, but I wanted more than that. I'd lost the people that had been my family and I didn't want to just be floating around meaninglessly. I wanted some kind of foundation, something that would root me, make me feel that I'd achieved something in my thirty-nine years. Yes, I wanted a family, a home. I wanted to build something, not just drift from day to day.

We may not have been lovers in the true sense of the word, but we were friends. And the week passed surprisingly quickly. Neil loved his island, and his enthusiasm was infectious.

The village where he lived felt strangely remote, almost like somewhere in the wild west, but I doubt if it witnessed many bar room brawls. It had one main street lined with low white cottages, a bridge over the river, a tiny church with a white pencil-shaped spire and a cemetery on the hillside, beside some standing stones. There was a pub and a post office with a shop.

"There used to be a bookshop as well," said Neil. "I remember my mum sitting there for ages with a cat on her knee and a cup of coffee."

"Your mum?" I asked. Oddly enough I'd never heard him talk about his family. But he'd moved on to another subject.

"There used to be a theatre here as well. It only seated about thirty people, but that closed too. By the way, do you fancy seeing a play?"

"What? Where? I thought you said the theatre had closed."

"Oh, it moved to Tobermory. One of my colleagues, Angus, is doing something there tonight. I said we might go."

"I've always wanted to go to Tobermory. Isn't that the place with the brightly coloured houses?"

"Yes, but it'll be full of tourists now it's the school holidays. I'll tell you what, I'll show you it from a different angle."

The drive was spectacularly scenic and horribly twisty. I just hoped Neil would keep his eyes on the road and not on any interesting birds flying over, as he negotiated a particularly sharp hairpin bend. Fortunately, he was also a very slow driver, so I didn't have that to worry about, though I did wonder whether the old car would make it up some of the steeper sections. Instead of taking the turning for the town, he went another mile or so and turned into a woodland park. Neil didn't seem too impressed by the number of cars that were parked there. I think he would have preferred it if we were the only visitors.

He was soon striding off down one of the paths that wound through the woods, binoculars round his neck as usual. Before long, we were clambering over fallen trees, squelching through boggy ground and clambering up alongside waterfalls. I was glad I'd brought stout boots as I struggled to keep up. Gallantry wasn't Neil's style. I couldn't see him laying his cloak, like Walter Raleigh, over a muddy puddle for me to step on. In fact, he didn't really make any concessions to the fact that I was much smaller and much less used to rough walking than he was. Or to the fact that I was female. It was part of what you might call his obliviousness, though I also rather liked that about him, the way I was just a person, a friend, to him, not some alien being of the opposite sex.

Soon we came to a lake surrounded by the woods, and then to my surprise we were on the edge of the sea. And across the bay was what looked like a toy town: a row of brightly coloured houses looking over a harbour full of boats, and a backdrop of mountains.

I turned to Neil in astonishment.

'Yes, that's Tobermory,' he said.

That evening, we watched the one-man show that his colleague, Angus, was performing, a sort of mixture of poetry and song. It felt strange to be with Neil in a public place. I always associated him with the open air and with wild places. After the show we joined Angus for a coffee. He was rather attractive in a sharp-featured David Tennant sort of way. Neil introduced me to him as his 'friend, Helen, from Hull'.

"Hello, Helen from Hull," said Angus in his soft Scottish brogue. They talked a bit about school, and I tried to imagine Neil in his smart jacket and tie, in the staffroom, teaching his class. I bet they loved him, even with his English accent. It was hard to imagine him raising his voice at them. And at the same time, I couldn't imagine them playing him up. He always seemed so calm and self-contained.

On the way home, I asked him if he enjoyed his job.

"Yeah, it's good," he said. "Better here than at the last place. The kids are all right. And the staff. But you know it's still work, a means to an end. I get to live here and that's what matters."

The next day we drove up from the village to some lochs we'd passed on the way to Tobermory. Surrounded by peaty moorland, they were very atmospheric but a bit bleak. I hoped we weren't in for a long birdwatching session, but instead, Neil led me up a path next to ruined cottage on the hillside beside the road.

"Where are we going?" I asked.

"We're climbing a volcano," he said.

It was a bit of a muddy trek up the hill, which didn't look much like a volcano to me, and the last bit was pretty steep, but then suddenly the path emerged onto a rocky ridge. Down below there was a dark loch, shadowed by the sloping sides walls of the crater. It was dramatic, romantic, like the scene for a novel by someone like Walter Scott. But I didn't feel like I was in a romantic novel. We were companionable, comfortable with each other. Often Neil would stride on ahead, in his own little world, scanning the sky with his binoculars, sometimes passing them to me so that I could see for myself. Though when a golden eagle flew over, there was no mistaking its size and majesty. Being up there felt like being in an eagle's eyrie, high above the world.

As we followed the path around the rim of the long-extinct volcano, a magnificent view opened up over the sea and to some islands.

"That mountainous one is rum," Neil said.

"Why?" I asked.

"No, that's its name: Rum. And the other ones are Canna and Eig and Muck. They're the small isles. The mountains on Rum are the Cuillin, not to be confused with the Cuillin of Skye." He'd turned into a Geography teacher again. What did that make me? His pupil?

Sometimes, though, I felt like I was much older than him. There was something boyish about his enthusiasm for the islands and for birdwatching. He could completely lose himself in these passions of his. But in relation to me I felt he was always reserved, always holding back.

One morning he asked me if I fancied a boat trip. I wasn't sure. I can get a bit queasy on boats, although I'd been all right on the ferry.

"We could go out to Fingal's Cave. The sea's calm enough, I think."

"Fingal's Cave? Like the Mendelssohn thing?" I started to hum it rather tunelessly.

"Yes, that's the one. Amazing basalt columns."

I had my reservations as we boarded the small boat that would take us to the Isle of Staffa. But then I looked around at the mixed selection of passengers, which included young children and some elderly people that seemed quite doddery on their feet. If they could manage, I should be able to. Though I think some people started to turn a bit green around the gills as we approached the island and the boat started to bob about rather alarmingly. What had Neil said about the sea being calm? The waves lashed against the vertical cliffs of the island, and I wondered how on earth we would get ashore.

But then I got my first glimpse of Fingal's cave and someone on the boat switched on the music, blasting us with Mendelssohn as we approached.

"It's a bit corny isn't it," said Neil.

"No, I love it!"

Somehow, we managed to disembark, climb up a ladder and follow the slippery walkway into the cave, the sea water lapping inches below. There was a handrail, but I wondered how some of the other passengers were managing. Then there were steep steps up the cliffs onto the grassy plateau on top of the island.

Neil was telling me about the puffins that flocked to the island in the summer. I asked him how he'd known about all this, why he'd chosen to come here, to Mull, to the Hebrides.

"I came here with my mum and dad," he said, "years ago when I was a teenager. Usually, we went to Skye because my dad was a climber, but one year we came to Mull instead. We stayed at a cottage in the middle of nowhere, by an old harbour. That's when we went to the bookshop with the coffee and cats."

"Did they come back here, your mum and dad?" I asked.

"I think they meant to. They didn't exactly get the chance."

And he told me how his father had died in a climbing accident in the 1990s when Neil was at university. Then his mum had fallen apart and, shortly afterwards, lost her life in a car crash. The way he said it sounded flat, unemotional, though I guessed he must have buried a lot of feelings.

"I'm so sorry, I had no idea."

"No, why would you? Anyway, I guess we're both orphans, aren't we?"

And that was when I found myself telling him about Jim. Not the whole story, not about the Gaul and the twin brother and everything I'd found out. I hadn't told anyone that. But I told him that Jim had met my mum on a one-night stand and that he never saw her again and didn't know she was pregnant until he met me last autumn.

"How did you meet up? What made him come looking?"

I told him about the newspaper article in 2007 and how Jim had eventually come looking for Linda when it was too late.

"How did you feel, finding out that he was your dad? Have you stayed in touch?"

"No, not really. I mean I saw him again, just the once, but it wouldn't have worked out. He was all right, though. I liked him actually. But it was too complicated."

And we left it there. But finding out about Neil's family explained a lot about him. The way he seemed so self-contained, self-sufficient, as if he didn't want to get too close to anyone again.

* * *

Another day we drove to a beach of pure white sand and a sea of turquoise blue. If it wasn't for the cold wind, we could have been on a tropical beach. I tried to imagine for a moment that we were on a honeymoon, imagined us sitting together, raising a glass as we looked into each other's eyes. No, it just didn't work. We were not those people, and our relationship was not that of lovers. I knew that Neil had quite other thoughts going through his head as he strode out onto the rocks, his binoculars trained on some distant black speck on the sea.

One day it rained, and I'd have been happy to stay in the caravan, reading. I was glad I'd brought my Kindle. Apart from the Tolkien, Neil had a number of fantasy novels, none of which were by authors I'd heard of. But most of his books were non-fiction: books on birds, geology, natural history. It was really quite cosy in the van when it rained, and I started to see why Neil liked it. However, he was determined to go out. He seemed impervious to weather, always pretty much wearing the same clothes, whereas I was always worrying about what to put on, what to take with me, what layers to add, which to remove. Soon we were walking alongside the sea loch, clambering over the slippery rocks, looking for some fossilised tree or other. I was cold and wet and as usual struggling to keep up with him. He didn't seem to have any awareness that my legs weren't as long as his. Once again, I thought that he didn't really seem to have much awareness of me as a separate person. I was just there. I wondered if he ever thought about me when I wasn't.

I think it was then that I realised that the saying isn't true, the one about no man being an island. Because that's what Neil is. He is an island. Self-sufficient and at one with nature. It doesn't matter to him that he won't have children, because he feels part of something bigger, the natural world, the environment. Neil is an island, on an island.

Although I shared his bed, I knew that I was just a visitor in his life, like the migrating birds that stopped over on his island. I knew I might see him again, or not. It would depend on which way the wind blew. And it wouldn't matter. He would be pleased to see me if I passed his way, just as he was pleased to see that egret passing through Spurn, but he doesn't need me. I will always associate him with cool northern coasts, wild open landscapes and salty sea air.

And somehow that clear bright air cleared my mind too.

CHAPTER TWENTY-TWO

A New Beginning

My trip to Scotland had clarified a few things for me. It was time for me to move on, to set off on my own journey, at last. Instead of listening to the sound of doors closing, I would try to open some new ones. Life could after all begin for me at forty.

I had quite a bit of money in the bank after years of living quietly at home, enough to put down a deposit on a house. Although there was more bedroom tax to be paid now that the house was seriously underoccupied, there was no problem taking over the tenancy. But I felt that as long as I stayed in my nan's house, I would never live my own life. It was time to put that too into the past.

I knew a lot of people on the estate from when I was at school, and I sometimes saw them around, but I hadn't really stayed in touch. Even though I worked and lived locally, I felt that our lives had drifted in different directions. A lot of girls in my year had had babies when they were in their late teens or early twenties. I'd see them pushing their buggies and then taking their kids to school. I'd never wanted that, certainly not back then. That was why I'd moved into town, had my own flat. I had more in common with Amy, although she came from a completely different background to me. Even at school, I was always the quiet one, the one who liked reading, and I felt like a fish out of water until I went to college and realised I wasn't some kind of freak. I didn't have to be loud and streetwise in order to fit in.

It was different for Amy in some ways. Her parents lived in a semi in the leafy suburbs. They obviously saw themselves as being a cut above people that lived on council estates. But as Amy once said, if you live in Hull you don't have to look back far into your family history to find some connection with Hessle Road and the fishing industry. Her parents expected her to do well and were pleased when she married a lecturer, but they didn't understand why they had chosen to live in such a draughty old house, full of books and second-hand furniture.

Sorting through my nan's possessions reminded me of doing the same with my mum's things, a few years earlier. Only then I had my nan to help me. I decided to make three piles: keep, recycle or throw away, but it was shocking to realise how little stuff there actually was. How little was left to show for nearly ninety years on this planet. She hadn't really created anything, apart from a lot of knitting before her hands became too arthritic. And that would hardly live on for future generations. What she had created was a loving home for mum and for me. I thought about how she had welcomed Mum back when she was expecting me, and how she had always been there for both of us. And now there was just me left. What had I made of myself to make it all worthwhile? It was like it had all come to a dead end, my nan's life and my mum's, and the dead end was me. I could feel the tears welling up, but I knew they were for myself, not for my nan.

I didn't believe in heaven, but if there was one, she would be there, making a cup of tea for everyone. If she could look down on me, what would she want me to do with my life? I could hear her voice saying, "I just want you to be happy, pet. That's all that matters."

But how to be happy?

I spent the summer house-hunting, and in September I moved into my own home. It was a small, terraced house with a front door that opened onto the street and a yard at the back. This part of the city near the University is popular with students, and it was easy to spot their shared houses with their overflowing bins. They always had a temporary, rather unloved air about them. I'd never experienced that whole student thing. Studying in my home city, I'd not left home until I was working and able to rent my own flat. Other houses in this part of the city were occupied by young couples, elderly people, and some decidedly odd-looking characters. But I was much happier there than on the estate. It was close to shops and bars and cafes, and actually just a few streets away from the house that Neil had shared with Dan. I wondered if Dan was still living there. If Neil sold it, would he be able to buy something on Mull? I doubted it, from what he'd told me.

Amy moved in with me for a while as a lodger, once she had sold her house and divided the proceeds with Richard. It helped with the mortgage, and it meant I had someone to go to the pub with and share a meal with.

She hadn't needed to move any great distance. The house they'd lived in wasn't far away, on the edge of the Avenues, lined with trees and huge Victorian and Edwardian houses with long walled gardens that backed onto the inevitable tenfoots. They were mostly the homes of teachers and lecturers, professional people, and arty types.

My house just had a small back yard, but I spent that September painting it white and I had plans for pots of flowers and trellises. Like all town houses, mine was long and narrow and a bit dark, the rooms stacked behind each other, the stairs steep and narrow, but I loved it. I bought a drill, put up shelves for all my books, stalked the charity shops for bits and pieces. I started to feel like a character in a book again. Or maybe in a romcom.

I bought a bike so that I could cycle to work and kept it in the narrow hallway, but I started thinking seriously about my job. As I approached my fortieth birthday in October, I started asking myself questions about my career. It was as if I'd sleepwalked through my thirties, and I didn't want to carry on sleepwalking into middle-age. I enjoyed working in the small branch library on Northfield, I knew my regulars and I had good relationships with the local schools, but did I want to stay there for ever? With so much happening in preparation for the City of Culture year, I wanted to be part of the bigger picture.

When a vacancy came up, I applied, and soon I was in a more senior role in the Central Library.

So, all in all, a lot changed in a short time. Looking back over the last year, I couldn't believe how much had happened, though I tried to look ahead and not backwards.

It all came flooding back to me however, around the time of my fortieth birthday. I heard more news about the Gaul mystery. Apparently, the Russian authorities claimed that DNA tests proved that the bodies in the cave were not in fact English after all. This seemed to satisfy the police and the Foreign Office, but not the surviving relatives of the Gaul crew.

Of which, oddly enough, you might say I was one, if my uncle had indeed been on board that boat. How strange to think that the nefarious Jack was my uncle, however you looked at it. And how weird that my dad, Jim, didn't even know that. He never even guessed that they were twin brothers, despite all his talk of doppelgangers. But I felt distanced from it all. Gone were those feelings of panic when I discovered what had happened. It didn't really affect my life as I was living it now, especially as I had moved away from the house in Northfield with all its memories of my mother and my nan. It started to feel like a story I'd read in a book.

And when the winter drew on, I lit the gas fire in its ornately tiled surround and felt mostly content. I had companionship, books to read, films to watch, and a home of my own.

But come the spring, I started to feel restless. Ever since that trip to Mull I realised that I wanted to travel in real life, to see more of the world. Until then, I'd mostly travelled within the pages of the books I read. Now I wanted to see the places that I had read about. And that was how I found myself in a plane, circling above Venice, waiting for a thunderstorm to pass so that we could land.

CHAPTER TWENTY-THREE

Venice

I'd come to Venice by myself. Feeling a bit nervous about independent travel, I'd booked a weekend package with a holiday company, so it was all taken care of. Bed and breakfast in a small hotel on the grand canal, flights there and back from my nearest airport, arriving early afternoon. It was like the trip to Mull was a practice run for this. I'd booked it after much deliberation late one evening after we'd been in the pub, and the next morning I wondered if I'd done the right thing. Suddenly everyone was telling me it was mad to go there in the summer. It would be heaving with tourists. It would smell of sewage. It would be too hot and humid. But I just felt that if I didn't do it then, I never would. And I wanted to travel alone.

The only problem was that it didn't include transfers from the airport to the hotel. I had been a little anxious about negotiating the train or bus, my Italian not being up to much, despite a bit of a crash course before I set off. Eventually, having looked at all the options, I decided to treat myself to a seat on a shared water taxi that would take me straight from Marco Polo airport to the hotel. I followed the signs through the airport until I saw the water lapping against the pier.

It was clearly a first-time experience for the other passengers as well. With some trepidation we handed our luggage to the driver and then stepped into the boat which was bobbing around rather alarmingly. As soon as we'd taken our seats, we were off bouncing across the sea. The thunderstorm had long finished but the sky was still overcast, and the sea was both grey and choppy. A couple of passengers started to look a little queasy, but for me it was exhilarating. Approaching the city in a speedboat made me feel like a movie star, like Angelina Jolie in *The Tourist*. In fact, most of my preparation for the trip had involved watching films set in Venice. When I should perhaps have been learning some Italian, I was studying Katherine Hepburn's outfits in *Summertime* and watching Dirk Bogarde's hair dye drip down his face in *Death in Venice*.

The speedboat slowed down as we reached the canals of Cannaregio in the northern part of Venice, nosing its way under low bridges and dropping off my fellow passengers at rather dilapidated-looking hotels. I was pleased now that I'd booked a room overlooking the Grand Canal. It had seemed like an extravagance, but I thought if I'm going to do this thing I might as well do it properly, and actually it didn't cost that much more. In truth I was a bit worried about what it would be like. Having seen the eye wateringly high prices of some of the hotels, I was worried that mine might be some awful dive smelling of sewage. On the other hand, the reviews had said it was good value: old fashioned but clean.

The driver helped me out onto the landing stage and passed me my luggage. The reception area looked promising anyway, with its marble floor and walls hung with tapestries. Huge chandeliers of Murano glass hung from the ceiling. I checked in and got the key to my ground floor room, which I entered through two heavy oak doors, one after the other. I'd been worrying that it might be swelteringly hot, so I was relieved to see that it had both air conditioning and a dehumidifier.

Other than that, it had a queen-size bed, an old-fashioned wooden wardrobe, a bedside table, a safe (for my jewels?), a shelf with a kettle, a mini-bar, and a small but clean ensuite shower room. An ornate glass chandelier hung from the ceiling. The rug was a little threadbare and there was altogether an air of faded splendour about the place. Not quite as swanky as the one that Angelina shared with Johnny Depp, but not at all bad. Especially when I drew aside the heavy brocade curtain and saw the view of the Grand Canal.

I quickly unpacked my clothes and then set off to explore, clutching the map I'd been given when I checked in. The double doors at the back of the reception led to a small courtyard which opened onto a narrow alleyway. I decided to ignore the map for the moment and just wander where my feet took me.

After a few turns, I found myself on a small bridge leading to a large square. Tables with brightly patterned tablecloths were set out under a sun canopy, Although the sky was still cloudy, it was warm. Aware suddenly of a great thirst, I sat down.

"Uno large beer, per favore," I said, mentally congratulating myself on not using Spanish, whilst reprimanding myself for not learning a few more Italian phrases.

The waiter gestured with his hands as if to confirm that I really did want a large one.

"Si," I replied. Did he raise his eyebrows slightly? I usually drank pints. A half was never enough by itself and what was the point of having to reorder? The waiter returned carrying a litre-sized glass tankard, like a German stein, and a bowl of crisps. I resolved to find out how to order a medium sized beer in future.

As I worked my way through the beer, I watched a depressed-looking young man leaning next to the bridge. Every time a family with children passed, he would take a lump of some jelly-like substance from the plastic bag in front of him and throw it to the ground. The lump of goo would form a ball that wobbled around for a few minutes. Occasionally a child would linger and watch, only to be dragged away by parents. I felt rather sorry for the young man, although he could have shown a bit more enthusiasm during the demonstration. And I certainly wasn't tempted to buy a lump of goo just so that he could make a sale.

Feeling more than amply refreshed, I continued on my walk. On the corner of one of the shabby buildings there was an arrow and a sign reading 'Rialto'. Following the signs took me along more narrow streets lined with shops, more turns down narrow alleys and over more bridges until I emerged into what was clearly a market square, leading onto the quayside. Ahead was the famous Rialto bridge, packed with tourists and lined with stalls selling tee-shirts, carnival masks, summer hats, keyrings, fridge magnets and other glittery souvenirs.

Across the bridge were streets with upmarket shops, selling leather handbags, fashionable clothes and designer glassware. I didn't even bother looking at the prices. I may have arrived by speedboat and have a room overlooking the Grand Canal, but I needed to stretch my hard-earned spending money over the three days of my city-break.

Arrows on the sides of buildings now pointed the way to San Marco, and I decided to follow them, although sometimes they would disappear for a while, and I would choose a right or left turn at random. Then the skyline between the closely packed buildings seemed to open up, and I was in St Mark's Square. Pigeons and tourists filled the piazza, while the colonnaded buildings stretched into the distance on either side, lined with tables and chairs.

What did Katherine Hepburn do? Ah yes, she had a glass of wine at one of the tables, listening to the orchestra. I'd been warned about the prices that I'd have to pay for the privilege of listening to the music, but how often would I get the chance to do this? I selected a table, ordered a glass of prosecco from one of the waiters in his white jacket and bowtie, and tried not to think about the bill. After all, I was paying for the view and the orchestra and the whole ambiance, not just for a drink. It was only then that I remembered that I'd already unintentionally drunk a litre of beer. No wonder I was feeling a little light-headed. Maybe I should have had a pot of tea and a piece of cake, like a lady. Oh well, I was on holiday and there was no one with me to criticise.

I watched a vendor present a delighted middle-aged lady with a bunch of long-stemmed red roses and then turn to her less-delighted husband to request payment for them. Katharine Hepburn, in her role as Jane Hudson, had been upset to see so many couples passing by when she herself was single. Well, that was over sixty years ago. Now no one needed to be half of a couple. It was just fine being alone in Venice. And who knew? Maybe I would meet my own Renato. Maybe, even now, he was sitting behind me, looking at my legs as Renato had looked at Jane Hudson's. I hoped not. Lecherous swine. I put on my sunglasses and took out my mobile phone to make a video of the view: the Campanile, St Marks's Basilica, the Doge's Palace, the pavement cafes, the clock tower, the arcades. All with the orchestra playing 'O Sole Mia' in the background.

All at once, the music stopped. The pigeons flew off. What was that distant rumbling sound? The clouds were rather dark and heavy. Surely it wasn't about to rain. As the waiters hurriedly gathered up the tablecloths, one of them darted to my table to present me with the bill. I gulped down the last of my wine, paid over my euros and joined the crowds now rushing to take cover under the arcade. Squashed in with a crowd of tourists, all elegance abandoned, I gazed in through the windows of Florian's cafe, where a few smug people sat on the plush seats under the ornate mirrors and gilded ceiling.

It shouldn't be too difficult finding my way back, I thought, leaving St Mark's Square, once the rain had eased off, and plunging into the labyrinth of narrow streets and alleys. Half an hour later, in a virtually deserted square, I had no idea where I was. Taking out the map, I tried to find a street name that matched one of the ones I could see on the side of a building, but it was difficult. I wasn't entirely sure which part of the city I'd wandered into, and the names on the map were all abbreviated. A light rain was falling, slowly soaking the paper. It was a good job I'd brought a folding umbrella. In the end I decided to pick someone who looked purposeful and follow them. The plan seemed to work. Gradually the streets became more crowded, the shops more plentiful. I must be approaching the Rialto area. My hunch paid off. Signs to the Rialto bridge started to appear and after crossing it, I was back in home territory, near the market. From now on it should be easy. Yes, here was the square where I'd drunk beer, and here was the bridge I'd crossed. Now it was just left and then right. Or was it left and then right? I knew I was near the hotel, but which alley did I need to turn down? It was now raining more heavily, and it was difficult to juggle umbrella and map at the same time. To make matters worse, the map was getting increasingly soggy and about to disintegrate completely.

A few yards ahead, I could see a covered section of the alley. Several people were huddled under it already. Joining them, I took out the damp map again, only to find that it was too dark to read it. I got out my mobile and tried to remember how to turn on the flashlight. It was only then that I realised how many people were doing the same. But it was hopeless. These alleys were too small to identify on the map. Not that I was worried. It was a sort of adventure, after all, and the hotel couldn't be far away. I set off again, back towards the square, but stopped to ask the first non-tourist-looking person I saw for directions. 'Just turn right,' he said. And yes, there it was.

As I entered the reception area through the double doors at its rear, I caught sight of myself in one of the enormous gilt-framed mirrors. Well, I don't look quite as much like a drowned rat as Katharine Hepburn did when she fell in the canal, I thought. But I came quite close.

After a refreshing shower, I wrapped myself in the bath towel and lay back on the bed for a little snooze. Before long I'd dozed off and fallen into a dream where the waters of the canal were rising outside my room until they started to seep in through the window. I woke with a start and noticed with relief that it had actually stopped raining and the canal was no higher than it had been. It was time to go out for something to eat.

I'd done my homework. Apparently, mosquitoes could be out and about once the sun set. And in the damp muggy streets after the thunderstorm, they would certainly be on the lookout for tasty human flesh. Carefully I sprayed herself with insect repellent. Then I looked at the bottle and realised that I'd used the spray that gave relief from insect bites, not the one that would deter them from biting. Should I have another shower and start again, or just use the insect repellent on top? And what about make-up? Should it go over or under the insect repellent? Then it was on with a long dress and a light jacket to cover my arms. What about my head? Should I wrap a scarf round my hair? I gave it a quick spray instead. Better safe than sorry.

I remembered Neil telling me that you had to wear a midge net over your head if you went walking in the summer on Mull. At least it had been too early for midges when I'd visited. I thought about Neil for a few minutes. We'd been in touch, of course, since I'd stayed with him, but hardly on a regular basis. And mainly he was just telling me about birds he'd spotted. He'd left an open invitation for me to visit, but he didn't exactly beg me to return. And I'd been busy with getting my house and making my plans. I definitely felt that it was a case of out of sight out of mind as far as he was concerned. I wondered what he'd make of Venice. Funny, I got the impression he didn't have a great urge to travel, though I think he'd done a lot of it when he was younger, after university. But now there was the whole green, carbon footprint thing about flying. And he wasn't particularly into art. I didn't really associate him with man-made places, just with nature and the sea. Well, Venice was by the sea. No doubt he'd have his binoculars out. But there weren't any fancy rock formations for him to wax lyrical about. It was all man-made. And he wasn't particularly into food either.

So where to eat? I headed back towards the square, carefully noting the sequence of left and right turns. Plenty of people were out and about, arms and legs uncovered, apparently heedless of the risk of mosquito bites. The shops were still open. In *Summertime*, Katherine Hepburn bought an antique Murano red glass goblet that caught her eye in a shop window. Inside the shop, she came face to face again with the handsome Renato, and such was the instant attraction between them that she was covered in confusion. I spotted some Murano red glass earrings for a few euros and decided to treat myself. The shopkeeper was slumped dejectedly in his chair. He looked and sounded like the most depressed man I'd ever seen, even more than the street vendor with his lump of goo. What sort of sale would cheer him up, I wondered? Not my cheap earrings, obviously.

Back in the street a much more enthusiastic Italian was trying to lure people into his restaurant. "Free prosecco, lady," he offered as I tried not to catch his eye. Why did I shake my head? Why didn't I take him up on his offer? I didn't like being rushed, that was why. I liked time to decide, to look at the menu, to check that it wouldn't be outside my price range. Maybe it would be best to return to the café I'd visited earlier, the one in the square, where I'd drunk an unfortunate amount of beer. The menu had looked pretty reasonable, with plenty of pasta dishes.

It looked cheerful and busy, the bright tablecloths glowing in the light of the sinking sun. I studied the menu. Of course, to sample the authentic taste of Venice, I ought to order the *spaghetti al nero di sepia*, with fresh squid cooked in its own ink, but I knew I wouldn't. What was the point of spending money on something I almost certainly wouldn't like? Instead, I played safe and went for the spaghetti Bolognese. Maybe tomorrow I'd be braver, or on my last night I could push the boat out a bit, if I had any money left.

After my meal, I decided to stay a bit longer. I ordered a Bellini, prosecco with fresh peach juice, to satisfy myself that I was having an authentic Venetian experience. Okay, it wasn't exactly Harry's Bar, but it was nice. A busker set up in the square to play his guitar. That was nice too. It added to the atmosphere. When he passed his hat round, I put my change in it, hoping he would continue, but then he left, moving on to another square, no doubt. For the first time, I felt a little lonely. It would be nice to have someone to talk to. Although if anyone did approach me, I would probably do a Katherine Hepburn, put on my sunglasses and pretend the other seat was taken. I began to feel self-conscious. Suddenly people seemed to be looking at me. I hurriedly settled the bill and headed back to the hotel, congratulating myself on not getting lost.

I could go back to my room and raid the mini bar, but that felt a bit sad. The evening was still young. There was a small bar just off the reception area, so I decided to order a night-cap. Disaronno. That sounded suitably Italian. I would have a Disaronno on the rocks and drink it on the balcony.

The lights of the palaces opposite were reflected in the water. Gondolas passed to and fro.

How strange, I thought, that the water can lap against the buildings here, and it's all fine, but it was a major disaster when it happened in Hull. I knew there was a big problem with Venice flooding and sinking, but it was as if it the city's natural state was to be semi-submerged. I'd heard that there was a bookshop in the city, in which the books were stacked in boats so that they could set sail when the waters rose.

Here was another city that had been deluged and learnt how to survive. But I couldn't help thinking just how far from my hometown I had come in one day.

I'm in Venice, I thought contentedly. I'm living the dream.

CHAPTER TWENTY-FOUR

An Encounter

On Saturday morning I piled my plate from the buffet table. Well, a good breakfast would see me through the day. To my surprise, the doughnut oozed custard, while the large croissant that I'd just spread with apricot jam turned out to be full of chocolate. I looked enviously at the people who'd bagged the tables outside on the balcony. A little bespectacled man was sitting by himself, scribbling away in a notebook. Maybe if I lived in Venice, I would be a writer and not just a reader of books, I thought. I resolved to get up earlier the next day and bag the balcony table before he did.

The sky was a cloudless blue and it was clearly going to be a perfect day. Especially for a visit to the seaside. I wanted to visit the hotel on the Lido where Von Aschenbach stayed in *Death in Venice*.

This time I had no difficulty making my way to the Rialto. If my sense of direction had failed me, my sense of smell wouldn't. The market was brimming with fresh fish and sea creatures of every description, carefully arranged on crushed ice. There was the squid that I'd so wisely avoided at the restaurant. As well as normal fish with eyes and fins and tail in the expected places, there were prawns and langoustines, and all sorts of other weird and wonderful briny delicacies. No wonder Venice had such a reputation for its fish. Beyond the fish market in its columned hall were other market stalls selling fresh fruit and vegetables, spaghetti, and salami.

After feasting my eyes, I crossed the Rialto bridge and made my way easily to St Mark's square, feeling confident now, a seasoned visitor to Venice. At the end of the piazza there was a line of gondolas and beyond them the vaporetto station. I bought my return ticket and was soon sailing the short distance past parks and gardens on my left and across the open sea to the Lido.

After disembarking, I followed the Granviale Santa Maria Elisabetta, which was overspilling with flowers, cafes and grand hotels. It was strange to see cars driving down the street after the traffic-free alleys and canals of Venice itself. At the end of the road, I turned to the right and there was the famous Hotel des Bains where Von Aschenbach had stayed, towering above the trees in its grounds, but sadly boarded up. Opposite was its own private beach, tastefully laid out with little huts and beach loungers. After checking out the prices, I decided to make my way to the public beach further along the seafront road in the opposite direction.

I passed a red open top bus that had been converted into a bar, playing loud music. Then a path led from the road, past a playground, basketball nets, an area where young men were playing volleyball, past a café and palm trees and down to the beach, where it became a sort of carpet and then ended. I slipped off my sandals, stepped onto the burning sand and then literally hot-footed it the considerable distance to the sea, where I had a ladylike paddle. I suddenly felt very pale and English beside the bronzed people cavorting in the sea and sunbathing on the beach. Some were just lying on towels; some had brought their own parasols. A few were using deckchairs or sun-loungers, but it was more like the haphazard appearance of an English beach, rather than the pristine ranks of sun-loungers at the Hotel des Bains. Despite my hat, the intensity of the sun on my head soon sent me back to the shade of a parasol at the beach café, where I sipped a Spritz and watched people. Yes, there were beautiful toned young people, but plenty of flabby people letting it all hang out in their bikinis or swim shorts. Families with children were carrying towels and beach-mats down to the beach. A short distance away, a fence separated the public beach from one that was a sea of parasols.

"Excuse me, is this seat taken?" The voice was lightly but oddly accented. But then of course there were people here of all nationalities. I looked up and tried to speak, but I'd just taken a gulp of my drink and I exploded into a coughing fit instead. "Are you all right?" he asked.

"Yes, fine. Yes, I mean, no. The seat's not taken, please sit down." I looked for my sunglasses to put on to cover my confusion and then realised I was already wearing them. "Sorry about that. Went down the wrong way. My drink I mean."

What a nightmare. Why had I lost the power of speech? Why was I even talking? I always do that when I'm nervous. I started waving my hands around and only succeeded in knocking over what was left in my glass.

"Let me get you another," he said. "It was my fault for disturbing you."

"No, no, it's fine. I don't mind being disturbed. Anyway, you didn't disturb me. I was just sitting here.

I couldn't possibly. Accept I mean. No please. Well okay then, thank you.' He spoke to the waitress in fluent Italian. Well, obviously he was Italian with those looks. But then his English was perfect, even if there was something odd about his accent.

"Are you Italian?" I asked, foolishly.

"Half," he said. "And half Scottish. I grew up in Glasgow. Though actually both my parents are Italian by heritage, you just have to go back a few generations."

Of course, that explained the accent. I found myself telling him about my trip to Mull. I'm not sure why.

"And do you live here now or are you on holiday?" I asked.

"I live in Milan, but I'm working here over the summer, in a restaurant. And as a tour guide."

Over the summer. Was he a student then? He looked young, but not that young.

He seemed to read my mind. "I'm doing a postgrad course in Milan. I decided the family business wasn't for me after all. Sorry, I'm Marco, by the way, or Mark. That's what I called myself at school, so I didn't stand out."

With those dark eyes and that olive skin, I'm sure he stood out amongst the pallid Scots, I found myself thinking. And thinking how nice his hands were, and the dark hair on his arms. And how very nicely his tee shirt fitted.

"And you are?" I realised he was looking at me, looking at him.

"Oh, I'm Helen. I'm just here for the weekend. Long weekend. On holiday."

"And you're here with a friend? Waiting for someone?"

"No, just me." I found myself blathering on about *Death in Venice*. Luckily, he'd seen it, so he knew what I was on about. It turned out he was into films, and art.

"That bit at the end," he said, "when Dirk Bogarde's just sitting on the beach by himself and the hair dye's running down his face. It's kind of funny and sad at the same time."

"I know," I said. "I keep meaning to read the book. It's only short. In fact, I brought it with me, but I haven't got round to reading it yet. Reading books is what I do, usually. I'm a librarian. Sorry, to be so boring. At least I'm not an accountant. Oh, you're not an accountant, are you?" He didn't look like one.

"No, I'm an architect, or will be. You don't look like a librarian," he said, and again I felt his eyes on me and hoped I wasn't blushing. "And I think it's great that you're following your passion. Everyone should do that."

Could he actually read my mind? Definitely blushing now. Oh, he was talking about books. "I don't know. There's a lot of time doing things that are nothing to do with books. It's getting to be more and more about IT. And sometimes I feel it's just about giving people somewhere warm to sit down out of the rain. And dealing with an invasion of school kids every now and again."

"A bit like being a tour guide," he said. "Or working in a restaurant. But this, this is life." He swept his arm to indicate the bar, our drinks, the beach, me. "In fact, this is perfect."

"Yes," I agreed, meeting his eyes for a moment. What was the matter with me? I'd normally be much more defensive than this if some strange man tried to pick me up at a bar. I'd pretend I wasn't really by myself, that I was waiting for someone, like Katherine Hepburn in that film. But with Marco I didn't feel threatened. I mean he was definitely giving me signals but not in a predatory way. And he seemed genuinely interested in what I had to say.

And we just stayed there talking. Until people started to leave the beach. He looked at his watch. "Work calls," he said. "What are your plans for tomorrow?"

I told him I was thinking of visiting the island of Burano.

"Right, I'll come with you. I've got a free day. Which is a rare event. That is, if you'd like me to."

"That would be brilliant," I said. "I don't really know how to get there." I told him where I was staying.

"Okay, I'll meet you at the Traghetti, where the gondolas cross the Canal. It's just near the Rialto market. Shall we say 10.30?"

As he left, he gave me a smile that made me want him to stay for ever.

I sort of floated back to the vaporetto station. Part of me felt like skipping and part of me was telling myself off. But what the hell. I was on holiday after all.

Back in St Mark's Square, I decided to distract myself with some serious sightseeing. I considered St Mark's Basilica, but then realised that the seemingly endless queue stretched right round the side of the building. No chance. The sun was still blazing down. Next to it, however, people seemed to be walking straight into the Doge's Palace. Twenty-five euros the poorer, I soon found myself in another huge colonnaded courtyard. In front of me, someone was complaining about having to hand in their bag at the cloakroom. I surrendered mine happily, glad to be rid of its weight.

As I wandered through the state rooms with their magnificent frescoes, I wished I knew more about art and architecture. At least, being alone, I had no one to complain if I took too long reading the information boards. Then, seeing a tour group with a guide, I attached myself to it loosely so that I could listen in. I suddenly remembered that this was what Marco did, as one of his 'holiday' jobs. Even thinking about it made my stomach do a funny little lurch. I imagined him showing me round, explaining everything in his lovely, weird Glaswegian/ Italian accent.

Meanwhile it was becoming increasingly hot and humid. I started to feel a bit muzzy, and I realised that there was a reason my bag had been so heavy: it contained my water bottle. As I stood in front of Tintoretto's vast Paradiso, I felt my head starting to spin with the jumble of colours, people, cherubs, angels, flowing robes, upturned faces, beseeching hands, naked chests, arms, legs, haloes, and ghostly faces in the background. The cool air and bare walls in the prison cells, across the Bridge of Sighs, came then as something of a relief. It seemed to be a one-way system, but as I followed the narrow passages, up and down spiral staircases, I began to think I was going round in an endless circle, never to escape.

I was glad when I found myself outdoors again, making my way back towards the Rialto Bridge. It was easy to spot the Traghetti, the gondolas providing a ferry service across the canal. To think I'd be sharing a gondola with Marco (and a few other people) tomorrow!

That evening, I returned to the same restaurant, the one in the square. I'd had enough excitement for one day, I thought. This time I noticed that the little writer man from the hotel was there, also by himself, still scribbling away in his notebook. He didn't seem to be writing long sentences or even words, just quick jottings, after staring at the page for a few minutes. Maybe he was editing what he had already written. I wondered what he was writing, and for a moment I was tempted to walk past his table and see for myself. But then I decided not to. I'd just realised that he'd seen me looking at him, because he raised his white hat in acknowledgement. I gave the slightest of nods and then buried my head in the menu to hide my embarrassment. Today I would have spaghetti carbonara. Tomorrow I would be more adventurous.

CHAPTER TWENTY-FIVE

Another Island

I could hardly sleep for excitement, and when I did fall asleep, I dreamt that I was trapped in a maze, surrounded by high walls, covered with paintings of strange half-naked figures that seemed to be mocking my attempts to escape. I did escape, by waking up.

It was still early so I seized the opportunity to grab the table on the balcony. Another perfect blue sky. I'd managed to avoid getting burnt yesterday, so it would be on with the Factor 50 again, the sunglasses and hat, and a cool cotton scarf to sling round my bare shoulders. Hopefully I could create a picture of elegance, in the style of Katharine Hepburn or Angelina Jolie.

My idea of visiting Burano came from the film *Summertime*. How did Renato describe it? *The island where the rainbow fell*. According to the receptionist, I would just need to head for the Rialto fish market, cross the Grand Canal on the Traghetto (where I would meet my own personal Renato!) and then walk straight ahead until I reached Fondamenta Nuove, where the number 12 vaporetto left for Burano.

How different the market looked this morning. All the tables scrubbed clean, the floor swilled down, and just a lingering aroma of fish. And beyond them the striped poles of the Traghetti, the gondoliers in their striped jerseys, and Renato, I mean Marco, there already, looking impossibly handsome.

He greeted me enthusiastically with a hug and a kiss and handed me into one of the gondolas. We paid our two euros and when the boat was full, the gondolier's dog settled comfortably on the prow, and we were paddled smoothly across the canal. Okay, it wasn't exactly a romantic gondola ride for two, but at least I could say I'd been on one.

A piazza on the other side, with the obligatory artist in residence, led to a wide street lined with shops. It was the most like an ordinary high street that I'd seen in Venice, although of course there were no vehicles. I'd been advised that our route led straight ahead, but I was glad I had Marco to guide me through the maze of bridges and alleys. I noticed that some of the alleys just led to a dead end with nothing that would stop you stepping into a canal on a dark night.

Here I was blindly following Marco. Was I being unbelievably reckless, stepping into the unknown? It didn't feel like that. It felt safe. But then I wonder how many victims of heinous crimes have said the same thing.

I emerged unscathed from the shady streets into the fierce sun and heat of the quayside at Fondamenta Nuove. The vaporetta number 12 was there waiting and people were already boarding. It was filling up rapidly, but we found a seat towards the back. As the water bus crossed the lagoon, I felt a trickle of sweat running down my back, and I was glad I'd tied my hair up. Then I spread my cotton skirt under me so that my thighs weren't touching the hot plastic seat, feeling pleased I was wearing a dress and not shorts, though perhaps I wasn't quite striking the elegant note I'd aimed at. Like the multinational tourists around me, I found myself alternately fanning myself and swigging water in order to keep cool. Marco sat still, looking mildly amused by all this activity.

We called at the glass-making island of Murano to drop off passengers and then coasted round the edge of Burano to the disembarkation point. Already, I could see the brightly painted houses for which the island was famous, as well as large areas of grass and trees.

Soon we were following the crowds through a narrow street with more tourist stalls and shops selling items made with lace. Again, there were no cars, just canals and boats, little bridges, street cafes and ice-cream parlours. A belltower leaned crookedly against the skyline. Then we escaped the tourists and wandered the back streets, where washing was drying on lines strung between the colourful houses and the conversation was all in Italian.

Following streets and canals at random, we eventually came across a tempting-looking café. Here were tables with parasols and some shady trees. We ordered drinks and sat watching the world go by. The café was on a corner where a canal flowed into the lagoon, so there was constant bustle of activity. Boats came and went, and a barge was loaded with crates of beer. I didn't envy anyone having to work in the heat.

It was good to just sit and watch lazily. I don't remember everything that we talked about, but I know we never stopped. Marco was easy company and the conversation flowed as smoothly as water.

Across the canal, a family were picnicking under a shady tree. Behind them, the houses were painted lilac and coral. The air was full of the buzzing of cicadas. Every so often a boat would discharge a tour group, their guide holding a flag for them to follow. Some were coolly chic and stylish, others overdressed for the heat. Some were garrulous and loud, others orderly and well-regimented. We tried to work out the nationality of each group of tourists, picking up clues from their clothing and behaviour. Then we'd eavesdrop on them to see if we were right.

"It's not fair," I said. "You've got an advantage."

"Why's that?" he laughed.

"Because you're a tour guide. Obviously. You spend all day looking at parties of tourists. I bet you can guess what nationality they are when they come into your restaurant too."

"Not my restaurant. I'm just a humble waiter."

"How come you don't sound more Scottish or more Italian?" I asked.

Marco laughed. "I sound a lot more Glaswegian when I'm back home," he said, "but I have to tone it down a bit when I'm over here. Otherwise, no one would understand me."

"Have your family always lived in Glasgow?"

"On my dad's side, yes. But my mum is Italian. That's how it is in Glasgow. People that have lived there for generations and people that are newly arrived. Then there's people that go back to Italy, so it's constantly changing, but it's a close community, and everyone's related to everyone else."

"I didn't even know it was a thing, being Scottish and Italian."

"You've not heard of Eduardo Paolozzi?"

"No."

"Jack Vettriano?"

"No."

"Paolo Nutini?"

"Well, obviously."

"It was the Italians who brought fish and chips to Scotland."

"In that case, you'd feel at home in Hull," I said. "But you'd have to try the pattie and chips."

"Fish patties, I'm guessing?"

"No, it's fried mashed potato. I suppose it's sort of potato served with potato. In a bread cake."

"Sounds pretty Scottish to me."

A boat drew up and two monks disembarked, dressed in brown tunics with cowls. I wasn't sure what I expected monks to look like, but I couldn't help feeling that there was something suspiciously un-monk-like about these two. Maybe it was the navy baseball cap that one of them was wearing. Together, we concocted an imaginary scenario where they were part of some crime syndicate.

Then a water taxi drew up. The smartly uniformed pilot was assisting a young man out of the boat. "He must be rich," I said, "to travel alone by taxi."

Instead of speeding off, the pilot sat down to wait. We speculated as to who the well-dressed passenger might be. In his white shirt and smart trousers, he wasn't dressed like a tourist, or at least not like the ones on the guided tours. He was just carrying a black leather man bag. Was he here for business or pleasure? Was he a film star? Why was he travelling alone? Maybe there was a connection with the mysterious monks.

We sat there, in the sunlight, in full sight of everyone who came and went. Plenty of witnesses, I thought, if he did intend to abduct me or worse. That hardly seemed likely, the more I got to know him. He was younger than me and carefree in his manner, but underneath it I had the sense that he was kind. It was strange but for the first time, I felt as if someone really saw me. I mean that he saw me as a separate person, took an interest in me, and made me see myself differently, as if I was worthy of interest.

I still didn't know much about him, but I was pretty sure he was single. It didn't feel as if this was a hole-in-the-corner situation. I remembered how Alan and I had lurked in the shadows, behind closed doors. But here, it was broad daylight. We took photos of each other on our phones and didn't worry about who was watching. Returning on the vaporetto, we held hands, and I wasn't even thinking about the heat.

Back in Venice, Marco took me to a restaurant I'd never noticed before, down a quiet side street, not far from my hotel. The owner obviously knew Marco and greeted us both enthusiastically. Then he showed us to a table in a courtyard hung with grapevines and flowers.

I told Marco about my unadventurous food choices on the previous two evenings, and he asked me if I would like him to choose for us both. There was a real pleasure in his eyes as he watched me eat, discovering new tastes and textures that were nothing like my previous experience of Italian food.

I knew we would end up going back to my room together. I think I'd known from the moment we met. And

I already knew what sort of lover he would be: tender, generous, taking time to explore me and to understand my body and what it was saying to him. The best of lovers.

CHAPTER TWENTY SIX

Departure

I had to be up early on the Monday morning, to be ready and waiting for the water taxi that would take me back to the airport. The little bespectacled man was waiting too and clearly wanting to engage in conversation, though I was fiddling with my phone in an attempt to avoid catching his eye. I didn't want to talk to anyone. But when we got into the boat, he sat uncomfortably close to me.

"Here by yourself?" he asked.

It was impossible to pretend otherwise.

"Stinks, doesn't it?" What was he talking about? I hadn't noticed the smell that Venice was infamous for. Then I realised what he meant.

"Oh, I quite like being by myself," I said, hoping he'd take the hint. He didn't.

"It wasn't supposed to be like this. It was meant to be me and the wife. Anniversary trip. Funny how you can be married to someone for thirty years and then realise you never knew them."

I wouldn't take the bait. I really didn't want to hear about his marriage, so I tried to change the subject. "Are you a writer?" I asked. "I wondered if I'd read anything by you."

He looked puzzled. "I shouldn't think so. A writer? What made you think that?"

"Your notebook? You always seem to be writing." Oh no, now it seemed like I was actually interested in him, especially now I'd admitted that I'd been watching him.

He laughed. "It's Sudoku. Do you do them?"

"Not really my thing," I said. "I always make a mistake and mess them up, so I just end up filling them in with random numbers, to make it look like I've completed them. Same with crosswords, but with letters not numbers. I prefer crosswords on the whole, though I'm not really a puzzle person." Why was I encouraging him? I think I was just glad of the distraction really, and he seemed harmless enough now that we'd got talking.

"The wife liked crosswords, not them cryptic ones, though. And wordsearches. Like chalk and cheese, we were. We liked different things, but I knew what she liked, and she knew what I liked. We knew each other. Well, I thought we did. And then one day she just says she's leaving. Says she's bored and she's going to travel. Well, I said we could travel together, when I retire. But she said I just didn't get it. She said I never wanted to go anywhere, just do my sudoku puzzles. Said I'd settled into wearing slippers and falling asleep in front of the telly. I said I thought that's what she liked. She said I never asked her what she liked. And then she left. Went off with a backpack. And I thought I'll show her. I can be interesting and adventurous. So, I booked this trip to Venice. Only it wasn't the same, coming without her."

He looked really sad. I was afraid he was going to cry. Weirdly, I hoped he wasn't wearing any mascara that might run down his cheeks behind his glasses. Then I remembered it was Dirk Bogarde's hair dye that ran, not his mascara, in *Death in Venice*. That made me smile, thinking about visiting the Lido and talking to Marco about the film. I wondered if I would ever see him again. We'd said we would meet again, but who knew? I thought about Katharine Hepburn saying goodbye to Renato and felt my own eyes filling up.

It took me by surprise when Sudoku man seized my hand and thanked me for listening. "You understand, don't you?"

Oh no, I thought, he's going to say his wife didn't understand him. But fortunately, at that moment our boat arrived at the airport.

Despite my best attempts to evade him, I kept on bumping into him as I went from floor to floor looking for check in and security. Was he going to be on my plane or another one that left at the same time? Please let it be a different one, I prayed.

I thought about Katharine Hepburn again, Renato running after her train with a gardenia in his hand. I pictured Marco running down the runway as my plane took off.

Then I pictured Sudoku man sitting next to me on the plane. Please, no, I thought.

Marco didn't come running down the runway, but neither did Sudoku man sit next to me. I had the window seat next to a couple who were preoccupied with each other, so I was free to think my own thoughts. The copy of *Death in Venice* was still in my bag, but I wasn't in the mood for reading. Like Von Aschenbach, I too had had a summer romance, but it existed in the real world and not just in my imagination. In the hot Italian sun, I had found friendship and, yes, passion. I'd felt like I was having my time in the sun at last.

CHAPTER TWENTY-SEVEN

What Next?

I had no illusions. It had been a holiday romance, and a very short one at that. But it had been intense. And nice. For a few weeks, I would lie awake, thinking of ways in which we could meet up again. I couldn't bring myself to let him go mentally. I imagined scenarios in which we were together, in which I moved to Italy, or he moved back to Scotland. I even tried to imagine us living together, getting married, but I couldn't. I could only imagine him seeped in the colours, sounds and scents of Venice.

We had promised to stay in touch, and he was true to his word. He sent me a photo of me sitting at a table, drink in hand, drenched in sunlight. *A lovely memory*, the message said.

I replied, keeping it light, whilst wondering to myself how long before our correspondence would fizzle out.

For about a month I felt the afterglow of my trip to Venice. Amy noticed it immediately.

"So, you enjoyed your trip then?"

"Er yes, obviously. What's not to like about a sunny weekend in Venice?"

"It's not just that though, is it? Tell me what's happened. You've met someone, haven't you?"

I don't know how she'd guessed. "Yes, but it's not going anywhere. Another holiday romance, that's all." I told her about Marco.

"And you're definitely not seeing him again? He sounds lovely."

"I don't see how I can. Shame though. You're right. He was lovely. But what about you? You're looking a bit more cheerful too."

"Oh, it's early days. Nothing to tell. Not yet."

Gradually I settled back into my routine. The trip to Venice and meeting Marco had shone an unexpected beam of sunlight into my life, as if a blind had been pulled up, or a shutter opened. But as the autumn drew on and my birthday approached, I started thinking again about that closed door. I was nearly forty-one and the chance of me ever becoming a mother was slipping further and further away. What would the rest of my life look like?

I looked at myself in the mirror. Hair still blond, face still relatively unlined, the face of a woman not young but definitely not middle-aged. My trip to Venice had confirmed that I was still desirable. But for how long? And what was the point in weaving fantasies around a holiday romance? I'd sleepwalked through my thirties, so why was I still wasting my time on unsuitable men?

I think I went a little insane after that. Although I never admitted to anyone else that I was trying to find someone to father a child, it was at the back of my mind all the time. I couldn't ignore what had now become a pressing need in my life. Every time I met someone of the opposite sex, I found myself assessing their eligibility. But how to meet the right sort of person? It's not so easy once you're out of your twenties. The idea of going out 'on the pull' didn't really appeal. That was how the whole affair with Alan had begun, and anyway Amy seemed to have something going on that she wasn't sharing with me.

Other people seemed to get results from internet dating, so maybe that was the way forward. At least I could weed out unsuitable candidates before really falling for them.

Creating my profile was the first hurdle. How should I describe myself? *Attractive single woman seeks handsome, intelligent man to father a child before it's too late.* Maybe not.

I didn't want to ask anyone else for help, because I was afraid it might smack of desperation, but I did listen in when people at work were talking, and that helped me find the most suitable dating service to give me some control over who I was speaking with. I also found some useful advice online. The first thing apparently was to know what I was looking for. Well, that bit was easy enough. I was particularly clear about what I wasn't looking for: *Married men, wife-beaters, and anyone about to emigrate need not apply.*

Then I had to choose photos. I really liked the one that Marco had sent me, but to use it felt strangely disloyal. I couldn't quite say why that was, but then I found out that sunglasses and hats were a no-no, which ruled out anything from Venice anyway. I decided that my long fair hair and green eyes were probably assets that should be on display. Marco had said I didn't look like a librarian, but I didn't want to look like some blond bimbo either. For a moment I almost gave up. This was too difficult and felt a bit demeaning, as if I was laying myself out like goods on a shop counter. But what was the option?

Living like a nun or entering the cattle market of the night clubs?

Then I had to write my bio. That was difficult. It made me realise how little I'd done with my life, especially in the seven years I'd spent living at home after the floods. Why hadn't I developed more interests during all those years of being single? It seemed a bit lame just to say that I enjoyed reading and watching films. But then, I was looking for someone compatible after all. There wasn't much point in making up a fake personality. And why had I travelled so little? Why had I always lived in my hometown? It was a bit depressing really, but I knew I wasn't that boring person that my bio seemed to describe.

Eventually however I was ready to launch myself into the world of internet dating. And after a while, the conversations started. And then the dates.

There are parts of my life that I'm happy to relive. The short time I spent with Marco gave me happy memories, even though it left me a bit wistful. I still smile when I think about my time with Neil on his island. But I prefer to gloss over the affair with Alan because of its repercussions and some lingering feelings of guilt and regret. And my attempts at internet dating are something I'd probably rather forget.

They weren't all terrible disasters, however.

Kevin was family man material all right. He was kind and sensitive and knew a thing or two about changing nappies. The proof was his four children that he went on and on about all the time. I didn't want to piggy-back on the back of someone else's ready-made family and messy divorce.

Then there was Steve, who sounded really interesting

online, but turned out to be so self-absorbed that I couldn't bear another hour in his company, never mind a lifetime together.

Ian was too flash. Always on about how much he spent on cars and shoes and fancy phones. I couldn't see him giving up any of that for family life.

Alex was action man. He wanted me to accompany him on kayaking and sky-diving trips. I felt that parenthood would definitely cramp his style.

To be fair, none of them measured up to Marco. Oddly enough, whenever I pictured family life, it was his face that I saw. He might have left his immediate family in Glasgow, but he seemed to have relatives all over Italy. He had talked so warmly about his nephews and nieces. I realised he was in fact my ideal man, being also amazingly handsome and attentive. But he was half a continent away.

Was I being too picky? Should I just have picked someone with good genes and gone for it, using them as a sort of sperm donor? No, I couldn't do that. I wouldn't have made Neil a father against his will. So why would I choose a random man? Also, I wanted to somehow break that pattern of absent fathers that seemed to run through my family history. If I had a child, I would want him or her to have a father, one that actually stuck around. And not one that got drunk and aggressive like my grandfather.

The problem was that instead of looking for companionship, romance or just plain sex (fancy sex even!), I couldn't stop wondering whether the men I dated were good parent material. I would try to picture us in one of those adverts that shows a wholesome sort of couple, walking through woods, each holding the hand of a small child. Or playing cricket on a beach. It didn't matter if the men that I met for drinks or meals were funny, clever, good-looking or charming. Some of them were some of those things. But it felt irrelevant.

Much as I tried to disguise it, I'm sure my desperation kept showing through. Was that why none of my dates really worked out? Or was it that all the men I met were fundamentally unsuitable?

It was when I was talking to Amy one day late in the autumn that I realised that I had actually become fixated with the idea of motherhood. We sometimes met up for lunch now that we were both working in the city centre. She was no longer lodging with me, having moved out during the summer. She now had her own flat, which she was sharing, bizarrely, with Richard. He'd come running back to her with his tail between his legs when things hadn't worked out with his bit on the side.

"I can't believe you took him back," I said, "after he'd walked out on you."

"Well, it wasn't quite that simple," she said. "But I could see he was really sorry. No, more than that. He realised he'd made a terrible mistake."

"Too right he did. Leaving you for that bitch. She must have known he was married when she set her cap at him…" I trailed off, only too aware that I was actually being a massive hypocrite. I'd never told Amy about Alan. That had been part of the fun, keeping it secret.

I suppose I'm good at secrets. Maybe that runs in the family. My nan had kept her secret about her twins, and my father had kept his secret about his false identity. Now I was keeping the secret about what I had discovered about my parents. I've always had secrets, even when there was no need for them. I had a secret diary when

I was a teenager. I wonder if my mum ever read it. Too late now to ask. Maybe it was because I was an only child that I just got used to keeping things to myself. When I met Alan and discovered he was married, I knew his secret was safe with me. Had I set my cap at him? I suppose I had, never for a moment thinking about the consequences. And it was worse really, because I'd found out he was a husband and a father, and I still continued to see him. But then it wasn't just me, was it? He'd been just as responsible for carrying it on as me, and he was the one betraying his partner, not me.

"But I still don't see why you took him back," I said. "After all, it isn't as if you've got children. I mean, how do you know he won't do it again?"

"I suppose you can never know for certain," she said, "but the thing is, Helen, I love him. There's never been anyone else. And I do actually believe that he loves me. And there's something else. I'm pregnant."

Of course, I gave her a hug, but I didn't know whether I actually wanted to shake her, to shake some sense into her. I was both happy for her and angry that she'd taken Richard back. And also, I realised, deeply jealous. It was as if she'd somehow betrayed me by joining the ranks of the Happily Married with Kids brigade. It felt so unfair.

But it wasn't unfair at all, I realised later. Amy had made her choices and I had made mine. And it was the realisation of how bitter I felt that made me reflect on what I had become.

I had started to believe that motherhood was the one thing that would bring me fulfilment, as if it would somehow make up for losing everyone else in my life. For all I knew, I might not be able to have children anyway. Maybe that abortion marked the end of my one and only chance. Or maybe I would fall in love with someone who wasn't fertile, and I wouldn't find out until too late. I realised that it was ridiculous to pin all my future hopes of happiness on motherhood. I had now turned forty, and it probably wouldn't happen anyway. And it wasn't as if I wanted a baby at any price.

However, when Amy invited me to spend Christmas Day with her and Richard, I made my excuses. I wasn't sure that I wanted to share their new-found marital bliss.

If I was a character in a film, I would have spent Christmas helping out at a homeless shelter, or with a motley selection of lonely people that I would invite to my home. But instead, I spent the day watching my favourite films, drinking Baileys liqueur and eating ice cream from the tub. And thinking.

CHAPTER TWENTY-EIGHT

2016

In the New Year, I decided to end my search for the perfect partner. I stopped the internet dating and instead, I started taking photographs.

I remembered something Marco had said, that art was about seeing. When I looked back at the photos I'd taken on my phone in Venice and Burano, I felt I could relive those sunny days. But why should I leave it there? Why not celebrate what was around me from day to day? It was as if it had needed those wonderful vivid colours to waken my senses. Maybe Marco had something to do with it too, encouraging me to try new tastes and ways of seeing.

As I started to take more photographs, I became more aware of my surroundings. I'd always thought of my hometown as rather grey, and I suppose it was, compared to Italy, but now I found myself noticing things like the shapes of the bare trees that I walked past every day, and the textures of their bark. I looked up and noticed the big skies and the flaming sunsets. Wandering round the town, I became more aware of the architecture: domes and gables, statues and murals. I realised that there were patterns everywhere, even in the mud imprinted by gulls' feet. I would often wander down to the pier or the old fishing dock, where I could take pictures of the River Humber in all its moods. I'm not a great reader of poetry, but we'd had a Larkin Festival a few years ago, to mark the 25th anniversary of the Hull poet's death. I kept thinking of Larkin's description of 'the widening river's slow presence.' The river had always been there in the background, but now more than ever I was aware of its significance in my life. I also photographed reflections of old warehouses in the still waters of Princes Dock and wondered why I had failed to appreciate my surroundings for so many years. Maybe you have to practise being a tourist abroad before you know how to become one in your own town.

As the winter continued, I took black and white photos, recording the patterns made by bare trees and railings, chimneys and windows. I found I could create atmospheric images, like scenes from a film, by photographing the cobbled streets and narrow alleys of the old town, beside the River Hull.

Eager to improve my skill, I started looking at books on photography and visiting exhibitions and galleries. On a weekend, I couldn't wait to get out with my phone and then with the camera I'd bought myself. I even found an evening class where I could meet fellow enthusiasts.

Sometimes I would post my photos on social media, sometimes I'd send them to newspapers and magazines in the hope of winning a competition or at least getting them published, and often I would share them with Marco, knowing that he would see in them what I had tried to capture.

Our correspondence hadn't fizzled out, as I feared and expected. Although the romantic side of our emails gradually trailed off, we ended up sharing more and more. In Venice, we had discovered each other's bodies. Now we were discovering each other's minds. I told him about my nan and losing my mum. He told me about visiting family in Glasgow over Christmas and how he missed them, but there was no way he'd have been happy in the family business. His passion for art and architecture was obvious. He told me that he would be spending some time in Barcelona in the spring, studying the architecture of Gaudi.

I'd never been to Barcelona, though it had been an ambition, ever since I read *The Shadow of the Wind*. I decided to reread it and soon it became a bit of an obsession. I'm not sure however that my fascination with the world of the novel was entirely healthy. It was all about raking up the past and exposing dark family secrets. It even contained a story that featured a relationship between two people who turned out to be half-siblings, unknown to them. I'd never given that storyline much thought when I'd read it before, being more interested then in the modern-day love story. But now it had a new meaning for me.

I discovered from the internet that such events are more common than you might expect and are becoming more so, with the use of sperm donors. But a marriage or even a sexual relationship between half-siblings is illegal. The article I read mainly focused on the health risks, due to the passing on of recessive genes. Well, at least I hadn't inherited some awful disease, but what if I had a child? Would they be at risk?

As the winter wore on, I became more convinced than ever that I was in some way doomed. Apart from my new-found interest in photography, the main light in my life was writing to Marco. I found myself using him as a sort of confidant. It was strange, considering that he was younger than me and his life was so far removed from mine, but maybe that was why I felt free to tell him things I had told nobody else. I found myself telling him about Alan and the abortion, about Neil, even about my attempts at internet dating. Though I did it in a jokey sort of way.

In a more serious moment, I even told him how much I had wanted a child. If I hadn't been so sure that we were now basically penfriends, I'd never have been so honest, for fear of driving him away. Admittedly, I didn't ask about his love life. He could tell me if he wanted, but I wasn't going to pry. And to be honest, I didn't really want to know. Writing to him was almost like keeping a diary, a way of validating and giving value to my single life. It was like I'd stripped naked for him again. In return, he opened up to me about his childhood, his worries and his ambitions.

His family had a restaurant business in Glasgow, but he'd never wanted to be involved in it. That would have been fine if he'd planned to become a lawyer or an accountant, but the only subject he'd really excelled in had been art. His parents had thought he would be wasting his time going to the Art School in Glasgow, so in the end he'd compromised by studying architecture there. It turned out to be the best decision he'd ever made. He became fascinated by historic buildings. There were plenty of those in Glasgow, but it was Italian architecture that really inspired him. Whenever he could, he would travel to Italy, using the network of family and friends that spread out from his close-knit community.

All of which was fine, but when he graduated with no job to go to, he ended up being roped into the family business after all.

Don't get me wrong, he wrote. *We're a close family and I wanted to do my bit. I didn't even mind being hands on in the kitchen, but the business side never appealed to me and that's what my dad wanted me to take over. I did give it a try for a few years, but then I realised I was becoming trapped. Like I was living someone else's life.*

Anyway, to cut a long story short, I found this Master's course in Milan that focused on architectural design and history, and I knew it was my means of escape. I knew I could earn enough money working in restaurants to keep me afloat, and then I realised I could use my knowledge of art and architecture in Venice to be a tour guide as well over the summer. It's the best decision I ever made, though I don't know if my family see it that way. I'd like to see them more often, especially now I've got all these nephews and nieces, but when I qualify and get a proper job, I should be able to afford to travel more.

One particularly long winter's evening I found myself telling him about Jim. The whole story, including the fact that he and my mum were half-siblings. I hadn't meant to, but once I started, it all came out. I didn't know how he would react. Maybe he would be horrified, shocked. He was so into family. What would he think about me keeping it all a secret?

But he was very kind. He told me that my mother and Jim couldn't have possibly known they were related. He told me that he had looked into it and that it was unlikely that any child I had would suffer medically. Most importantly he reassured me that I had done the right thing in keeping it to myself, though he agreed it must have been hard.

I also told him about my strangely mixed feelings regarding my uncle, who I was now sure had gone down with the Gaul. From Jim's point of view, he was just a bad lot, but now I knew he was one of my nan's lost boys. Maybe if he hadn't been brought up in a children's home, he might never have messed up his life the way that he did, never robbed Jim and never ended up on the Gaul. But then, if that hadn't happened, my father would have been on the trawler instead. I suppose it's impossible to unravel time and wonder what would have happened if one thing had been different. If my parents had known they were half-siblings, they would never have spent that night together, but then I would never have existed. Thinking about it made my head spin, made me feel a wave of confusion rushing over me. I found myself thinking again about what it must have been like when the trawler went down into the icy water with all those men on board.

In return, Marco told me a story from the war that I'd never heard before. His great-grandfather had come to Glasgow in 1920, along with many other Italians driven from southern Italy by drought and famine. He'd soon moved into the café trade and had a thriving business and large family when the second world war broke out. Then Mussolini declared war against the UK and that was when everything changed. His sons, being British nationals, were conscripted into the army, but he himself was interned as an enemy alien. He was being taken to Canada when the ship, the Arandora Star, was torpedoed, and he was one of many that lost their lives.

Meanwhile his wife, Marco's great-grandmother tried to manage the business with the help of her young daughter, but they were subjected to abuse by the friends and neighbours who had once been their customers.

Marco had only heard this story many years later from his grandmother, the young girl who had helped keep the café running whilst she and her mother dealt with the news of Alfonso's death. She had been an important figure in Marco's life, just as my nan was in mine, and had died ten years ago when Marco was at university.

It was strange to find these parallels in our lives, that I had imagined to be so different from each other. I realised how little I knew about history and decided it was time to do a bit more research.

I started with the Arandora Star, the ship that had been transporting Marco's great-grandfather to an internment camp in Canada. It turned out there were over seven hundred Italian internees on board, of which over four hundred lost their lives. Ninety-four of these had been living in Scotland and most were middle-aged or older. The more I read, the more shocking details I discovered. Apparently, many of the Italians suffered horrific injuries caused by glass falling from the mirrors in the ballroom where they were sleeping. A ballroom? What was this ship, the Titanic? Although it had originally been a cruise ship, it had been painted grey to look like a warship and hadn't displayed a red cross to show that it was carrying civilians. I'd discovered when I was trying to find out about lost trawlers that many of them had also been requisitioned during the war. Not the Gaul though. That had been brand new, supposedly unsinkable, like the Titanic.

Some of the information I was looking for was only available from the National Archives, and I didn't fancy a trip to Kew, but it transpired that the work had been done for me. Someone had uploaded lists of everyone on board. I wondered which of the Italians from Glasgow was Marco's great-grandfather. All their names were there, their dates of birth, their birthplace in Italy and their place of residence in the UK. More than twenty were from Glasgow and there were even a few from Hull. Many were in their fifties and sixties, the heads of families who'd been left to manage without them.

It was claimed that some of the details had been difficult to obtain because they were subject to an eighty-five-year embargo, much longer than the usual thirty or fifty years. Was there something that the authorities wanted to hide? I thought about all the rumours surrounding the Gaul, the suspicion that it had been used for spying, the accusations of a cover-up. But the trawler had gone down in the seventies, not during the war. Things must be different in wartime: corners cut, a compromise with the truth, the need for propaganda.

I soon became intrigued by the story, quite apart from its link with Marco. I've always been like this. Once I get interested in something, I have to find out everything about it. I suppose that's why I became a librarian. Because as well as my love of reading, I understand the thirst for knowledge. When my curiosity has been aroused, I just have to keep digging. Wherever it leads. As I discovered when I started looking into my own family history.

There were lots of claims and counter claims about what had actually happened on board the Arandora Star. Claims that the internees were fighting among themselves, that the Italians had been afraid to jump overboard because they couldn't swim. And claims that sons refused to leave their injured fathers, that there were too few lifeboats and life jackets, that the military guards were untrained, and that the evacuation was impeded by the barbed wire that had been erected to keep the internees below decks.

I wondered what happened to those who were lost. Were their bodies ever found? And what happened to the survivors?

I read that many of the bodies were washed up and then buried in the Hebrides, the islands of Barra and Islay, as well as on the mainland of Ireland. I wondered if any had found their way to Mull. The injured were taken to a hospital, but fit survivors were taken to Australia on board the HMT Dunera. Such a long way to travel. It was hard to imagine that these men were such a terrible risk to the war effort that they had to be shipped halfway round the world.

But then I thought about my nan, and the bombs that were falling on Hull every night when she was still a teenager. All those lives lost, and all those homes destroyed.

* * *

It was so easy to say that it was all in the past, but there were daily reminders that such horrors continued, even in 2015.

In September, all the newspapers had been full of images of a toddler washed up on a beach in Turkey. And I think for a lot of people, me included, it had suddenly brought home the awful reality of people fleeing from Syria. Earlier in the year, eight hundred refugees had drowned on their way to southern Italy from Libya. People trying to find safety in the very country that Marco's family had left due to famine.

Now it all swirled round in my mind. The thought of people forever on the move, seeking safety or being taken away, being shipped across treacherous seas by people-smugglers or by governments, like a giant wave of humanity rolling around the world.

One day I'd been taking photographs of the old pier that juts out into the River Humber. It was here that Jim had taken the ferry to Lincolnshire, the morning that he'd missed boarding the Gaul. Opposite the pier, at the other side of the entrance to the dock leading to the marina, I noticed a statue that I hadn't seen before. Most of the statues around Hull were of important figures: Queen Victoria standing guard over the toilets in Victoria Square, the gold-clad King Billy riding his horse in the marketplace, Andrew Marvell outside his old grammar school. But this one showed a family: a man standing, one hand placed on the back of his wife who is sitting, holding the hands of a little girl in a smock, still a toddler, while an older boy plays with a lobster. It commemorates all the families that passed through Hull on their way from Northern Europe to the New World, over two million between 1836 and 1914.

How strange, I thought. I'd always thought of my home city as somewhere fixed, somewhere that people were born and then stayed, as I and my family had done. Yes, people went to sea, but they always came back, unless the sea took them. But for these migrants it had just been a staging post on their journey, before they caught the train to Liverpool and then the steamship across the Atlantic. I realised that Hull isn't a place apart, but one that is caught up in the great sea of migration.

CHAPTER TWENTY-NINE

Barcelona

In the spring of 2016, Marco asked me if I'd like to meet up with him, in Barcelona.

It was a casual sort of invitation, and I wasn't sure on what basis we'd be meeting, as friends or lovers. I didn't want to assume anything and get caught out, so I decided to book myself a city break, with a hotel included, and take it from there. I felt I'd become much more confident at travelling alone since that journey to Mull two years before. So much had happened since then. I'd heard from Neil occasionally, but he was never one to send chatty emails. Usually, it was just a brief message to tell me about a rare bird he'd sighted. As far as I knew, he pretty much stayed on his island. I suppose he had no family to visit, and he'd obviously made friends up there. What travelling he did was by ferry to other Hebridean Islands, Lewis and Islay, for the birdwatching.

I remembered Islay as one of the places where the bodies from the Arandora Star had been washed ashore. I doubted whether Neil would approve of flying abroad for a holiday. I couldn't really imagine him in a Mediterranean setting. He seemed to belong to the muted colours of the north. Then I thought about that beach of white sand and turquoise sea that we'd visited in Mull. But even then, there had been something austere and northern about the bay. In my memory, Neil would always be associated with mist and rain, remote beaches, boggy mountain paths and peaty lochs.

As I looked at the different hotels in Barcelona, I realised that my budget meant I'd have to choose between something a little seedy in the city centre or something more luxurious on the outskirts. In the end I opted for a four-star high-rise hotel with a rooftop swimming pool, in the Diagonal de Mar quarter, close to the sea. With its glass tower, it couldn't be less like the buildings in the wartime setting of Zafon's book, but I'd never stayed in a luxury hotel before, and I was looking forward to the experience.

My taxi from the airport delivered me to my hotel late in the evening. I'd eaten a meal on the plane, a sufficiently novel experience for me to actually enjoy it. I'd poured the tiny bottle of wine into my plastic glass and drank a little toast to travel and being independent. Checking in at the hotel was somewhat intimidating, especially when I realised that most of my fellow guests seemed to be businesspeople rather than holidaymakers. It was too late to try out the rooftop swimming pool, so I made my way straight to my room. Sharing the glass-sided lift with a stranger, I wondered whether I should say something to break the awkward silence, but then I decided to focus on the view of the traffic streaming up and down the Avenida Diagonal so as to avoid catching his eye. I couldn't help thinking it would be the perfect hotel to pick someone up. I wonder how many chance encounters in this lift led to drinks in the bar and nightcaps in bedrooms.

Businesspeople travelling alone, detached from their everyday lives. Who could blame them for finding a bit of company to ease their loneliness?

But what if they were married? I thought about Richard and felt indignant at the thought of men having a sneaky bit on the side. Then again, it probably wasn't just men that did it. And who was I to judge?

Opening the door to my room, I again had that feeling that I was a character in a book or a film. Everything was streamlined and modern. From the windows I could see across the lights of Barcelona to the mountains beyond, silhouetted against a deep turquoise sky. It was a far cry from the gothic gloom of the books, in which it always seemed to be raining or snowing. I didn't know how things would turn out with Marco, or how much time we would spend together, but I resolved to visit as many locations as I could from *The Shadow of the Wind*. I wouldn't let my happiness or fulfilment be dependent on someone else. And I had my camera with me.

I'd bought a small guidebook, which included a fold-out map. I knew that the Cemetery of Forgotten Books was an invention of Zafon's, but I managed to locate the gothic quarter and the Placa Reial, the restaurant Els Quatre Gats and the Montjuic Cemetery. I would try to take the blue tram up the Avenida Tibidabo and find the mysterious mansion, the Angel of the Mist.

As I pored over my map, I realised it was getting dark already. I should maybe draw the curtains, although it seemed a shame to shut out that view. Only there weren't any curtains, or blinds. No worries, I thought, I'm so high up that no one can look in, and got into bed. Only then I realised I could see people passing along the glass-sided corridor that ran along the outside of the hotel at an angle to my room. If I could see them, they could see me. It struck me that my room wouldn't be ideal for a romantic tryst, unless we wanted an audience. Hurriedly, I turned off my light and slipped under the covers.

Maybe it was the strange bed, or the sense of being in a goldfish bowl, but I lay awake for a long time. I kept wondering how it would be with Marco. Being by myself in a hotel brought back my memories of Venice. I remembered how I'd lain awake the night after we'd met. That same excitement was washing over me now, in waves of heat. And then there was the night he'd shared my bed. I allowed myself to relive that memory in all its detail, imagining he was here now. Maybe if I held that memory in my thoughts, I would dream we were together again.

Instead, my dream took me back into the world of *The Shadow of the Wind*. The library where I worked was somehow also the Cemetery of Lost Books with its glass roof and at the same time it was this hotel with its glass walls. I was travelling upwards and upwards in a glass sided lift to the very top of the building, looking down over a sea of books, spiralling stairs and passages, and then suddenly I realised I was trapped, that the ascent would never stop, and I banged against the glass side of the lift. In slow motion, it shattered, and I felt myself falling, falling...

CHAPTER THIRTY

Exploring

I woke with a start. Light was already streaming through the window. Why were there no curtains or blinds? I pulled the cover over my head, but it was no use. There was no chance of getting back to sleep, so I decided to explore my room. It was definitely a lot more luxurious than my room in Venice, even if that had overlooked the Grand Canal. The mini bar was well-stocked with beer and bottled water. The bedroom furniture was sleek and functional. The ensuite washroom gleamed from the other side of a glass screen. Again, there didn't seem to be much privacy. I started pressing each of the many switches on the wall to see what different lighting effects I could achieve, hoping that I wouldn't inadvertently call room service. To my surprise, and relief, I discovered they operated two sets of blinds for the window: a translucent one to screen out the glare of the sun and a heavy one to create full blackout at night. Another heavy blind screened off the washroom. Of course!

Marco wouldn't be free until the afternoon, which meant I had plenty of time for exploring. I began with the hotel. Although it was still early, the sun was shining so I decided to start with a swim in the rooftop pool. The pool side sun loungers were still empty, and there was no one swimming. I floated on my back, looking up at the clear blue sky. Whatever else this trip might bring, it was worth it just for this. When a large middle-aged man in a too-small pair of Speedos loomed up beside the pool, I made a speedy exit and headed for the sauna. It was already occupied however, and I didn't fancy another awkward experience like the one in the lift.

Having breakfast in the hotel didn't appeal to me. It wasn't included in the room price and was probably horribly expensive. Nor did I fancy sitting by myself amongst the business types that seemed to be the main clientele. Instead, I found a café on a nearby corner, where I ordered a coffee and churros. Then I walked past more hotels and a shopping centre to the seafront. The road ended at the Forum, a sort of cultural festival site, but I could see the beach on my right stretching endlessly into the distance, punctuated by rocky jetties projecting into the Mediterranean.

A refreshing breeze was blowing from the sea, and I was pleased I'd decided to walk along the soft sandy beach rather than take the metro to the city centre. It was very different from the beaches along the Yorkshire coast that get completely covered by the incoming tide. Here the sea seemed to know how to keep its distance. I'd read that the sand had actually been imported from Egypt when the seafront was regenerated for the 1992 Olympic Games. I wondered what it had been like before.

I'd read in my guidebook that this area used to house a shanty town built by immigrants fleeing from misery and hunger in Andalucia. That ever-rolling wave of migration had obviously swept over this city too. The people who lived here were later rehoused in apartments as part of the big clean-up of the seafront, but it hadn't necessarily been an improvement for the residents. One of them described the new apartments as a 'vertical shantytown'. That was something I could relate to. I remembered my nan talking about the demolition of the so-called slum housing on Hessle Road that was at the heart of the fishing community in Hull. She and her family had been lucky to get a proper house on Northfield. But there were others that were rehoused in tower blocks or the notorious maisonettes on the estate. Shoddily built and damp, they may have had indoor toilets and bathrooms, but they were plagued by vandalism and eventually demolished.

Feeling the sand between my toes and the spring sunshine on my shoulders, I couldn't help feeling I'd come a long way from Northfield. I had a professional qualification, a good job, a home of my own and independence. And here I was in Barcelona on my way to meet my lover. Or friend. I still wasn't sure which, but it felt good anyway.

The walk turned out to be further than I thought, and I was relieved when I finally caught sight of the giant copper fish sculpture in the distance. This was where Marco had suggested we meet up, as he said it would be impossible to miss. He was right. It towered above the shops and cafés, golden and glittering in the sunlight.

By this time, my feet and my head were feeling the effects of the long walk in the sun, and I feared that I wouldn't present the picture of cool composure that I'd hoped for. How would Marco greet me? How should I greet him? I still wasn't sure what to expect. It had been nearly a year since we had met, despite our long correspondence in the meantime.

But I needn't have worried. It immediately felt so natural that we should be together. And all our conversations online made me feel that I knew him so much better than before. As we sat at a table in the shade, sharing a drink, I found myself telling him about the hotel and my confusion over the blinds.

"I thought it would be like being in a goldfish bowl, with everyone looking in on us from the corridor," I said, and then stopped, realising I'd made the assumption that he would be there with me.

"You didn't need to book a hotel," he replied, and then he too stopped too, as if he was as unsure of me as I was of him. In the pause that followed, we both looked at each other. Then he added, "Your hotel does sound a bit classier than my digs, though."

We sat there for a long time. It reminded me of the time we spent in Burano, under the sunshade outside the cafe next to the canal. We had talked and talked then, as we did now. Afterwards we wandered hand in hand along a promenade lined with palm trees, beside a pristine beach, and then through the narrow streets of Barceloneta. It was in the old houses here, Marco told me, that the fishing community used to be based. The gypsy community had also lived here in another shanty town, all cleared away as Barcelona turned its face back to the sea and made itself look presentable to the rest of the world. In memory of the old days, a sculpture had been built on the beach. It was like four blocks with windows stacked randomly on top of each other, looking as if they were about to fall over. Marco told me it was called *L'Estel Ferit*, the Wounded Shooting Star, but I couldn't see why.

Being with Marco, I felt a new lease of life, no longer footsore and weary as we made our way past the statue of

Columbus on top of its sixty-metre column. It reminded me a bit of the Wilberforce monument in Hull, but it must have been a lot taller because it was almost impossible to photograph from close up. In any case, I wasn't really thinking of photography right now. I did get my camera out to photograph the living statues as we walked up the Ramblas and through the bird market. It was fun doing the whole tourist thing, especially with Marco at my side, but he also knew how to find little out of the way places to eat and drink, away from the crowds.

After wandering round the narrow streets of the gothic quarter, we took the Metro back to my hotel. I don't think we'd stopped talking all evening. At some point, he'd opened up about his past. I think I'd been telling him about Neil and how he always ate out of tins.

"You obviously liked him though, or you wouldn't have travelled all that way to see him on his island. I've never even been to Mull, or Oban for that matter. We didn't really do that hiking over the mountains stuff in my family. I think Loch Lomond was the furthest we got to the Highlands. Though I think Lucia would have quite liked to see a bit more of Scotland."

"Lucia? I don't think you've mentioned her?"

"We met when I was working in the family business. She was in her twenties too, but she'd just moved to Glasgow, not been brought up there like me. She was proper Italian, if you know what I mean. There's still loads that do that, come to Scotland looking for jobs. Especially from the south of Italy. There's really bad unemployment there, even if you're a doctor or lawyer. Well, of course, she got welcomed into the community and she came to the restaurant, and we started dating. I think I was so in love with the idea of Italy by then that I thought I was

183

in love with her. And she was the same, except that she was in love with Scotland. I wanted to learn more Italian and she wanted to improve her English. In the end we decided to use English for everyday stuff and Italian for the romantic bits."

"So, what happened?"

"Well of course my mum and dad thought she was perfect. A good catholic Italian girl and a doctor too. But I felt like my life was getting planned out for me. Before I knew it, we were engaged and there was a big family party, and I think it was then that I realised I'd never escape if I went along with it. It was around the time that I started thinking of moving to Italy. Of course, it was the last thing she wanted. And when I talked about being a student again, she was asking if I expected to live off her salary, and what if she wanted children, had I thought of that? Well, I hadn't. I was still in my twenties, and I was still trying to work out what I wanted to do with my life. It wasn't that I didn't want children. I just needed to find out who I was first."

"So, you split up?"

"Yeah, it was kind of messy. We tried the whole long-distance relationship thing, but it didn't really work. Then she announced she'd met someone else, another doctor of course, and that was that."

"Oh, I'm sorry."

"What? Nothing to be sorry about. I thought at first she'd broken my heart, but then I realised it was more my pride that was hurt."

"And after that, was there anyone else?"

"You tell me," he said.

CHAPTER THIRTY-ONE

Temptation

Marco had to work the next day, but I had my own plans. I was still on a mission to find more of the locations from *The Shadow of the Wind*. Marco wasn't a great reader. He preferred art and films, but he advised me how to travel by train to the Avenida del Tibidabo. A subway took me to the bus stop for the famous Blue Tram. Squeezing onto the crowded vehicle, I made sure I got a seat near the window. As we climbed up past the grand houses that lined the street, I tried to spot the Angel of the Mist, the mansion that is at the centre of dramatic events in the novel. When the tram reached its terminus in the Placa Dr Andrieu, I stopped for a coffee in a café that looked down over the rooftops of the city. It was hard to imagine that Barcelona had been at the centre of the Civil War in the nineteen-thirties. My hometown still had bomb sites until quite recently. But both cities had lived through war and survived.

After my coffee, I tackled the next leg of my journey, the funicular railway that would take me to the top of Mount Tibidabo. It ascended steeply through the wooded hillside, emerging near the old amusement park. It was easy to spot the red aeroplane flying high above the mixture of old and new rides, but I didn't go on any of the rides. I don't have a great head for heights or speed. And I was having to watch how much I spent. Not only that, but to me it felt like a place for children. Or lovers.

I had read in my guidebook that Tibidabo was reputed to be where the devil tempted Jesus, according to local legend. I wasn't sure that all the kingdoms of the world could be seen from this mountain, which at five hundred or so metres was surely a hill not a mountain. But it was a lot higher than the extinct volcano I'd climbed with Neil on Mull, although much less wild.

I wondered to myself whether I'd been sent here to be tempted. It was certainly tempting to imagine a life with Marco in a city bathed in sunlight. I'd been happy just reading about foreign places until I'd started travelling, but now my world seemed rather small and monochrome in comparison to the places I was discovering.

I remembered that one of the temptations of Jesus was to fling himself down from the pinnacle of the temple. Above me, at the very top of the hill (or mountain), rose the Church of the Sacred Heart. Its silvery white pinnacles soared into the sky, topped with a huge statue of Jesus. To me it was a fantastical building, like a Disney fairy-tale castle. But underneath it was a quite different building made of dark yellow stone, which I discovered was the crypt. I passed through a mosaic arch into an elaborate interior decorated with colourful mosaics. High up in the ceiling above one of the altars was a picture of a ship being tossed in a storm as it headed towards a grand domed palace arched over by a rainbow. I stared at it for ages. What was it trying to say? It felt like there was a message that I needed to decipher. Did the ship represent the Gaul? Was it a palace of dreams? Was the rainbow a promise of happiness? But what if the ship got wrecked before it reached the shore? I felt myself drifting into a state of unreality. Maybe it was the scent of incense. I needed to get some fresh air.

I followed the steps up to the terrace in front of the main church. It was time to take some photographs. That was, after all, what I had come for. And to find locations from the *Shadow of the Wind*.

I no longer felt infected by the air of gloom and despair that the dark themes of the novel had originally inspired. On the contrary I felt strangely free and light-hearted. Much as I enjoyed being with Marco, I realised that I was also happy doing this, enjoying my own company, taking photographs. I didn't feel like a part of me was missing, just that when I was with him, there was something extra.

For some reason I thought about Jane Eyre and how she builds an independent life for herself before she finally returns to Rochester. Maybe one day, there would be a place where Marco and I would be together. Or maybe our paths would lead in different directions. At any rate, it was the time to enjoy the here and now, not to worry about the future.

Later in the day we met up at the Miro gallery in Montjuic. I'd wanted to visit Montjuic anyway because its cemetery featured in *The Shadow of the Wind*, and I'd spent an hour or so wandering along its paths and terraces that wound between the elaborate monuments, before I was due to meet Marco. But what was dark and gothic in the novel was bathed in sunlight that reflected blindingly off the white marble, making me relieved to be wearing my sunglasses.

The old fortress appeared in the book as a sinister place that contained dark secrets, but it was now another tourist attraction. I looked up at the aerial tramway that linked the castle with the Barceloneta beach, flying high above the Port Vell. I couldn't think how it could have operated when the castle was the scene of imprisonment and torture during the Civil War. When I asked Marco about it, he told me that it had rusted away until the regeneration of the Barcelona seafront in the 1990s. It made me think about Hull and its old warehouses that were now restaurants and bars, its old disused docks that had been turned into a marina.

"You must come to Hull, sometime," I said to Marco, "though it's not quite on this scale. But you could try the pattie and chips."

"And you must come to Milan and try the ossobuco," he replied.

I wondered what Marco would make of my home city, when he seemed so at home in these European cities, full of amazing art and architecture. He had a way of noticing things that I wouldn't have seen if he hadn't pointed them out to me. What would he see in Hull that I had missed?

In the Miro gallery, the way he talked about the paintings and sculptures helped me to see them with fresh eyes. I loved the primary colours and bizarre shapes, but I couldn't imagine them looking the same back home. They seemed to belong here in Barcelona with its Mediterranean light and complicated history. I reminded Marco of what he'd said in Venice, that art is about seeing. "Do you see me differently after looking at all these weirdly shaped women?" I asked him.

To be honest, it was difficult for me to look at my surroundings when I was with Marco. I wanted to learn every feature of his face, every line of his body, for when we were apart.

That evening I looked at our limbs entwined on the bed, his olive skin next to mine, pale and freckly.

"To look at us, you'd think I was the Scottish one," I said.

"Well, at least there's a good chance we're not related," he replied.

CHAPTER THIRTY-TWO

Learning to See

I had asked Marco to tell me about Gaudi, because I knew that he had come to Barcelona to study his architecture.

"I shan't tell you; I'll show you," he said. "Today, if you have no other plans, we'll do our Gaudi tour of Barcelona."

"No other plans, but will there be a lot of walking?" My feet were feeling the effects of all the walking I'd done over the last two days.

Fortunately for my feet, it was a day of hopping on and off the Metro, as Marco took me to see various buildings designed or renovated by Gaudi. We started with the Casa Batllo. I wasn't really sure what to make of it. It looked like a perfectly nice tall building with balconies and green shutters. I really liked the colourful mosaic on its walls, but then there were all these twisting curving shapes that had been added: columns shaped like bones, balcony railings like masks. I told Marco it looked a bit sinister to me and he laughed. "It was known as the Bone of Contention when Gaudi added his finishing touches to it."

"I'm not surprised," I said. "What's next?"

Our next stop was the Casa Mila. "It's known as *La Pedrera*, which means 'the stone quarry'," explained Marco. I thought I could see why. There was something massive and solid about it, but it was at the same time kind of floaty. I realised I didn't really have the words to describe architecture. Just like the previous building, it was all curves.

"The straight line belongs to men, the curved one to God," said Marco.

"Did you just make that up?" I asked.

"No, Gaudi did," he replied.

"But all that twisted metal on the balconies doesn't look very heavenly to me. It reminds me of barbed wire."

"Well, our next stop should be more heavenly. We're going to church."

I'd obviously heard of the Sagrada Familia before. It looms up on every website or book about Barcelona. But seeing it in the flesh (in the stone?) was something else. In fact, I found it quite overwhelming. I usually think of cathedrals as being calm, majestic places, but this place was completely weird. Was Gaudi a genius or was he completely crazy? Before long, my head started to spin with the insane amount of decorative detail, overspilling every surface. It was too ornate, too much to take in.

Marco sensed that I was beginning to droop. "Don't worry," he said. "No more buildings. We'll stop for lunch and then we're going to a park."

We took a bus to the Parc Guell, and I thought what a relief it was to be with someone who knew his way around the city and its transport system. Although it was also full of fantastical structures and sculptures, the park felt strangely refreshing. Maybe it was the absence of traffic as we wandered along the terraces and walkways, or maybe it was the flowers and greenery spilling over the walls, but I no longer felt overwhelmed as I had before. Yet as we sat and rested on the serpentine bench inlaid with multicoloured mosaic, I felt as if I was in some kind of dreamscape. The terrace looked down over the city and beyond that to the impossibly blue sea.

Was this really my life? It all seemed unreal. For some reason I found myself thinking of that bit in Jane Eyre when she is about to marry Rochester, unaware that he has a mad wife in the attic. It was all too perfect. This attentive, good-looking man in this exotic other-worldly place. It was impossible to imagine him being part of my normal life.

I tried to imagine him in my little terraced house, having a beer in my local pub, and I couldn't. He was somehow too handsome for Hull. He belonged here, or in Venice, not in my world. I knew he had grown up in Glasgow, but I couldn't picture him there either. Maybe it was because I'd never been there myself, except for passing through on the train. I had no mental image of what his life had been like. His home, his family simply didn't exist for me. I feel like that about places I've never visited, people I've never met. They just don't seem real. Although oddly enough, I have no difficulty imagining a character or a scene when I read a book.

'So, what's next?" I asked.

"I thought you'd had enough Gaudi for one day."

"No, for you, I mean, when you finish your Masters."

"Back to Milan," he replied. "I've been offered a job already."

Milan, Paris, Rome, London. Those cities were always listed together. Never with Hull. I think I had always known that he would never move to Hull, but what I realised then was that I would not be moving to Milan, either. I couldn't tag on to his life, any more than I could keep up with Neil striding over his Scottish moorland. And what's more, I didn't want to.

Once upon a time I would have loved to escape from Hull, but I no longer felt trapped in my own life. I'd bought a house and found a job I loved. It was exciting to be part of the plans for the City of Culture year, part of the regeneration of the city where I belonged, with all its history and all my family history. I'd developed a deep sense of belonging and a desire to make a difference.

The realisation that we would be going separate ways made me feel a little sad, just as you feel sad on the last day of a holiday, but I was determined to make the most of the time we had left. I didn't need to run, like Jane ran from Rochester, just to accept it for what it was.

But a bit of colour would be missing from a world without Marco.

CHAPTER THIRTY-THREE

Waiting

Back home, I threw myself into my work. It was an exciting time, a real buzz starting to build in preparation for our Year of Culture. It was fun to feel a part of something so special, and I enjoyed working with other people and organisations to make things happen. All through my life, I had heard people apologising for coming from Hull, making fun of its accent, talking about the deprivation that followed the collapse of the fishing industry. The city was always coming top of the wrong sort of lists: worst schools, worst housing, worst place to live. But that wasn't how it felt to me. And I'd met plenty of people who'd come to Hull to study and then stayed, so it couldn't be all bad. But now, there was a real sense of pride starting to grow.

I did my best not to think of Marco, cutting down on the emails we exchanged, making sure I kept it light. But even while I was busy with work, I had the strangest feeling, as if someone was tugging at my sleeve for attention. I tried to ignore it, but eventually I gave in and asked myself the question directly.

I think I knew the answer even before I did the test. We had taken precautions, but we weren't as careful as we might have been. And now this. I knew of course that I would keep this one. In fact, I was more afraid that this tiny flicker of new life might be extinguished before it had time to grow. For a while, I just kept my secret to myself, as if exposing it to daylight might be too much for it.

As I said, I'm good at secrets. I kept postponing the moment when I would make this one public. First, I would wait for the first twelve weeks to be up, because after all it might come to nothing. Luckily, I wasn't nauseous, just more hungry than usual. And my usual drinking companion, Amy, was breast feeding her baby, so there was no one to notice I was off the booze.

I guess, without meaning to be, I'd been a little standoffish with her little girl. Maybe I kept my distance because I was so frightened of rousing that deep sense of longing in myself. I would just make a joke of it and say I was no good with babies, as I handed her back to Amy with a sense of relief. Even though I saw her as my best friend, I'd never confided in her about my feelings of broodiness. I suppose it was a form of self-protection. And then once I knew she was pregnant I didn't want her to suspect me of any hint of jealousy, so I encouraged her when she talked about me being as free as a bird with my single lifestyle and my holiday romances. It hadn't been too difficult to avoid her once she'd had the baby, and I genuinely hadn't wanted to get into discussions of childbirth and breast feeding. Now all that had suddenly changed, but I was afraid that I might give myself away before I was ready.

Then I thought I might as well wait until the pregnancy began to show. Unlike Amy who had soon ballooned to twice her size, I remained quite neat, and I was able to get away with slight alterations to my wardrobe.

Why was I so slow to tell anyone? It wasn't that I was unhappy or uncertain about what I wanted. On the contrary, I felt a deep sense of joy. As the summer rolled into autumn, I imagined the baby slowly ripening within me like a fruit.

I wasn't worried about what other people might think about my single status. That was none of their business. Times had changed from when my nan and my mum had fallen pregnant. I knew that it could be tough financially and career-wise for a single parent, and no doubt there would be difficult times coping emotionally. But the question was whether I would have to manage completely by myself. Much as I told myself that I didn't expect anything of Marco, at the same time I was afraid to tell him. I wanted to say that I hadn't tricked him into becoming a father and that he was free to walk away. But I didn't want to know for certain that it would happen.

The longer I left it, the harder it became to tell him. I wished now that I'd told him the moment I'd found out, or even suspected that I was pregnant. Then at least I'd have known his feelings and got it over with, when it was still just a possibility. But now it was a certainty and one that was growing rapidly.

How could I put it in an email? Since Barcelona, my emails to Marco had become shorter and shorter, as I tried to avoid the one subject that filled all my waking thoughts. I think he was hurt at first by what he must have seen as coldness, and maybe he thought I'd lost interest or moved on. I'd gone from sharing my innermost thoughts with him to writing about the weather and the preparations for the City of Culture. How could I now tell him that I was expecting his child?

I found myself thinking about my nan and how she had written to her sweetheart in the Merchant Navy to tell him that she was pregnant, never to hear from him again. I wondered how her life might have turned out differently if he had stood by her and married her as soon as she was old enough. Who knows? Maybe he was killed in the war, and she would have been left with her two sons anyway. Would her parents have supported them, or would she still have given them up for adoption?

But none of that helped with telling Marco.

It was around this time that the annual fair came to Hull. I used to love Hull Fair when I was a child. Even though we lived out on Northfield Estate, we always used to visit the fair. If you'd asked me my favourite time of the year, I think Hull Fair would have ranked higher than Christmas. My mum must have saved for ages to give me the best time when we visited. I think that was a tradition especially for fishermen's families, even though I never grew up with a dad in the fishing industry, and we never experienced that three-day millionaire thing, when money would be spent like water. There was still a feeling that it was a special time of year, and we'd spend as much money as we could find, even if we couldn't really afford it. I think that same mindset was handed down through the generations.

As the bus went up Anlaby Road, I used to look out of the window to see if I could spot the Big Wheel and to watch out for any signs that we were close: a child carrying a balloon or a fairy doll, someone eating candyfloss or carrying a goldfish in a bag.

Then there would be the walk down Walton Street with its fortune tellers and its stalls selling candyfloss and brandysnap, fish and chips, nougat (or nugget, as we called it). Father Christmas would always make an appearance, even though it was only October, and then there used to be a street preacher railing against sin and blasphemy. Eventually we'd reach a gap in the stalls lining the road and enter the fair itself.

When I was a teenager, I was allowed to visit the fair with my friends. It was the subject of much anticipation and speculation, often about boys. Who was going, and on which night, and who were they going with? Then when we arrived, there'd be groups of boys and groups of girls, hanging onto each other's arms to avoid getting separated in the crush. The young men operating the rides would flirt with all the girls, and we'd egg each other on to try the scarier rides. Sometimes I would lie awake worrying about it in advance, because I wasn't as daring as I pretended to be, but I could never admit it. The next day at school, it would be a point of honour to brag about which rides we'd been on.

I suppose I carried on going to the fair right through my twenties with friends and boyfriends. It was just something you did if you lived in Hull. But in recent years I'd given it a miss.

Now that I was living within walking distance, however, I felt the urge to return. I would go late afternoon when it was getting dark enough to appreciate the lights but not too crowded. Approaching Walton Street from the opposite direction felt strange. This end of the street felt quite different. Instead of the long lead-in of stalls, there were children's rides right from the start. I watched the families enjoying themselves, feeling a mixture of excitement and sadness. Excitement that I would be bringing my own child to the fair before long, but a certain sadness that their father probably wouldn't be going on the dodgems with them or watching as they went round on the teacups, or the galloping horses. I thought about the Tibidabo Amusement Park and its red plane flying hundreds of metres above the city. It was only a matter of months since I was there, but it felt as if my world had pivoted on its axis.

I bought fish and chips from Bob Carvers and ate them as I walked along the street. Then I stopped outside the brightly painted caravan of Gypsy Rose Lee ('descendent of the Original Gypsy Rose Lee'). I don't believe in fortune-telling, but for a moment I was tempted to join the queue. What might reading my palm tell her and me about my future? Did I really want to know what my heart line would say about my love life? Probably not. Would she be able to tell me the sex of my child? Perhaps she would. Though I could find that out from my mid-pregnancy scan later in the week. In the end I just bought some brandysnap and fudge to take home and decided that I would tell Marco my news after I had the scan. At least I would know then if everything was all right with the baby. That gave me a good excuse to put it off a few more days.

There were other pregnant women waiting for their scans. Most had their partners with them. One young girl had her mother there. I felt self-conscious about being so obviously by myself and had decided to say that my partner was working away, if I was asked. But then I thought that maybe I should get used to being a single mother, dealing with things by myself.

"Everything seems fine," said the sonographer. "Did you want to know the sex of your baby?"

I'd already decided to say yes. For some reason, I thought it would make it easier when I was telling Marco, though I don't know what difference I thought it would make.

I had to go back to work afterwards, but I couldn't concentrate. As soon as I got home, I decided I would just have to come straight out with it.

There's something I've been meaning to tell you for some time, I wrote, *but I didn't know how to tell you or how you will react. I'm expecting a baby and yes, you are the father. I know it's not what either of us was planning and I totally understand if you don't want to be involved. I've made my decision to keep the baby, but it's up to you whether you want to play any role in her life. I don't ask anything of you. I honestly didn't mean it to happen, but maybe it was just meant to be.*

And that was all I could think to say.

Several hours later, there was still no reply. I realised I'd been pacing up and down the room, wondering how he'd react. Maybe he would be angry that I hadn't told him before. I found myself asking myself why I'd left it so long. Or maybe he'd think I'd tricked him somehow into fathering a child. There again, I hadn't wanted to use emotional blackmail, but had I sounded too cold? Should I have told him how much I wanted him to be a father to my child? I realised I'd eaten a whole packet of ginger biscuits without even realising, while I'd been pacing up and down the room. I couldn't focus on making myself a meal. The excitement I'd felt at finding out I was going to have a little girl had turned into a feeling of being overwhelmed by waves of panic. Stay calm for the baby, I told myself. Breathe.

His reply when it came was short.

I wish you'd told me before. I must see you. Just checking flights xxx

Was he angry then? Was that why he'd taken so long to reply? But there were kisses. Everyone puts kisses on their emails. But three? Maybe, he'd just been busy with work. He was coming to see me. What did that mean? He wished I'd told him before. Before what? Had he met someone else? Is that why he needed to see me? Oh my god, oh my god. I didn't know what to think, how to feel. Then another email:

Any chance of you getting down to London? Are you well enough? I can get a flight to Gatwick early tomorrow, but it'll have to be a flying visit. Flying because I'll be on a plane, haha.

Was I well enough? I'd never felt better. And he'd made a joke. That had to be a good sign. I could hardly check my excitement as I checked train times. Luckily it was Saturday the next day and there were through trains from Hull. I could get a day return on Hull Trains, arriving at Kings Cross before 9 if I caught the first train of the day.

CHAPTER THIRTY-FOUR

Another City

Believe it or not, I'd hardly ever been to London. I'd visited the British Library as part of my training and I'd been to a couple of shows with my mum, but that had been years ago. I'd never gone by myself, and I was quite excited at the prospect, enough to distract me from the confusing feelings I had about meeting up with Marco. I decided to stop trying to second guess what he was thinking. After all, I would find out soon enough when we met up.

I took a book to read on the train, but I couldn't concentrate. There was a fluttery feeling in my tummy, and I wondered whether it was the baby moving or just my digestive system reacting to an early start. I gazed out of the window and eventually allowed myself to drift off to sleep, secure in the knowledge that I wouldn't need to change trains. I knew that the fun would really begin when I got to Kings Cross.

Marco would be travelling by train from Gatwick, but he didn't expect to arrive at Victoria Station till mid-morning, and he would be flying back in the evening. It suddenly occurred to me that he was possibly completely mad. Who goes on a daytrip to London from Milan? The whole thing was insane. I'd been too busy booking my train tickets and poring over maps of the London Underground to think about it properly. But then it was the only way we were going to meet up, and the cost of London hotels was truly insane.

I'd worked out that I could travel on the Northern Line from St Pancras to Victoria, but I had loads of time to spare, so I left the tube at Green Park and walked. I looked at my map of London. Mayfair and Piccadilly were close by. It was like walking across a Monopoly Board! Should I pop into the Ritz for coffee? Maybe not. The colours of the autumn trees in the park were calming after the noise and crush of the Underground. I'd never done the whole tourist thing in London, I thought, as I ogled the Victoria Monument and Buckingham Palace. I must travel more in future. Then I suddenly remembered. Well, I would travel with my daughter, I resolved.

Rather than having to hang around in the station if one of us was delayed, Marco had suggested we meet at Westminster Cathedral, which was only a five-minute walk away. It occurred to me that I'd never been to church so much as I had with Marco, although I think that had more to do with architecture than religion. None of my family had been churchgoers, but from what I'd seen of English churches they were a far cry from what I'd seen in Italy and Spain. So, Westminster Cathedral was a bit of a revelation.

At first, I thought Marco had meant Westminster Abbey, which I'd seen on TV. My nan used to love watching royal occasions. That would have cost a small fortune to enter, I'd discovered, unless I was attending a service. Unlike the Abbey, the Cathedral was a little bit tucked away and easy to miss. And it was free to enter. But inside, I was blown away by the glittering gold and mosaics. It felt magical. I remembered how I'd felt overwhelmed in the crypt of the Tibidabo church and how I'd searched for meaning in the picture with the rainbow. Maybe I'd already conceived by that time. But this felt strangely peaceful. No one was looking at me. No one approached me. Some people were praying, some just resting, others walking around. I sat down and felt myself becoming drowsy again, despite sleeping on the train.

When someone sat down next to me, I knew without looking that it was Marco. We exchanged a few words in whispers and then left to find a place where we could talk and have lunch.

"Why didn't you tell me?" I knew this would be the first thing he would ask. I tried to explain, hesitantly at first and then the words came tumbling out. By the time I'd finished I was in tears as I tried to explain that I thought he might not want anything more to do with me.

"But how could you think that? I thought you'd met someone else."

"And I thought you'd met someone else."

And then we were both crying. And I knew it would be all right.

CHAPTER THIRTY-FIVE

A Reunion

The sun is glittering on the white masts and hulls of the boats, their jangling mingling with the cries of seagulls. A busker is playing the violin nearby, families walking past, tourists of all nationalities seeing the sights. Flowers spill from hanging baskets. And I'm sitting at a table beside the marina, waiting.

This is Hull and it's enjoying its moment in the sun.

On a bitterly cold New Year, I had squeezed into the crowd that filled Queen Victoria Square to watch the lightshow that would launch the City of Culture. With tears rolling down my cheeks, I watched the story of Hull projected onto the buildings. The walls of the City Hall appeared to blaze with the fires of the Blitz, while the Art Gallery was engulfed in waves, carrying drowning fishermen into the depths.

That is the history of Hull and it's my family history too. A story of tragedy and courage, of loss and survival. The city lives in my heart and my memories and will always be a part of who I am, its stories woven through my family.

Yes, the past is the past and although it is part of who I am, I shan't be ruled or restricted by it. I'm free to travel where I want.

But whatever happens, I shan't be travelling alone.

There is someone new in my life. Isla already has her father's dark eyes and his winning smile, but right now she is sleeping next to me in her pram. She is fresh and new, her future a book waiting to be written, its pages still blank. I don't think our fates are written in the stars.

If this was a book, how would my story end? *Reader, I married him?* Or would it be a story of how I'd learned to live my own life without relying on someone else?

In real life there are no endings, happy or otherwise. But I've come to realise that life is full of new beginnings.

Sometimes I ask myself those 'what if?' questions. What if Jim had never met my mum in Baileys that night? What if he hadn't met his twin brother the next day in the George? What if the Gaul hadn't sunk?

But there's no point in asking what if. Because to undo those events is to undo my own existence. Does this mean that I believe in fate? Was it fate that these meetings and coincidences happened?

Who knows? There may be such a thing as fate, but that doesn't mean we're not free. The past has made me who I am, but it doesn't need to control my future.

Marco was with me in Victoria Square on New Year's Day. He had travelled to Hull on the train after spending Christmas with his family in Glasgow. He couldn't be with me for the birth of our daughter, but he has met her since. Now that he is working, he can afford to travel more frequently and to support us in other ways. We live in different countries, and our work will keep us apart much of the time, but he is a part of both of our lives.

I know it will be difficult, but I won't be the first to bring up a child by myself. The wives of trawlermen and those women whose men were fighting in the war had to manage while their husbands were away. And when they never came back. At least I have a job that I love, and I will find a way to combine work with caring for my daughter. There is still so much more to be done in this city. I want her to be proud of where she is from, all of it.

Marco says he wants Isla to grow up knowing her father, and so do I. As for my relationship with him, that particular door remains open. He plans to introduce his daughter to his parents and of course his brother and sister and their children, her cousins. And then I will meet them too. It's a daunting prospect after coming from such a small family: all these relations that extend from Scotland to Italy. As I look at the Humber Bridge in the distance, stretching from north to south, I think of all the family ties and histories that form bridges between countries. For the moment, my country has turned its face away from the continent, but I feel more connected than ever, in this city that has always reached out from its widening river to the sea and beyond.

I can sense the wind blowing through the open doors and windows of my future, like the sea breeze that sets the international flags flying above the marina. A new chapter is being written in my life.

I remember my mum telling me that there's no such thing as 'having it all'. She said that it was just something they said in magazines. No one gets the man and the child and the career that they want. She said she was happy just having me and doing a job that she enjoyed.

I think about Amy. She has her daughter too, but I wonder if she will she ever really trust Richard again. We see each other, often. She still calls Marco my 'holiday romance' and reminds me playfully that her brother, Max, is still available. It's good to share my experience of motherhood with a female friend who lives nearby, and I'm sure that our daughters will grow up as friends.

And after becoming a mother, I made another decision.

I see him approaching from a distance. He is walking into the sun and shielding his eyes, so I realise that he can't see us. It gives me time to study him as he approaches. He seems to have aged since I last saw him. Over his lifetime, he has lost so much and has carried so many secrets. I too have experienced loss, and I too must carry secrets about the past. But the past is the past. And who knows what the future will bring? As he draws closer, I notice a spring in his step that wasn't there before, and as I see his face more clearly, a sparkle in his eye.

At that moment, my daughter wakes up, 'Isla, meet your Grandad Jim,' I tell her.